"I didn't put you down as a romantic, Tess Hope."

Josh grinned fiercely. "Maybe I should think again."

A romantic? That was the last thing she was, surely. "Don't be such a fool." She stepped gingerly from the flooded cellar. "I'm a realist. But I do have to...feel something before I can — commit myself to lovemaking." She was glad he couldn't see her face.

He was close behind her, though, and his voice was soft. "And how often have you 'felt something,' Tess?" There was a pause. Why should she tell him? It was none of his business. "How often?" They reached the top of the stairs and emerged into the light and warmth of the house. "Not often — am I right? Not very often at all."

WELCOME
TO THE WONDERFUL WORLD
OF *Harlequin Romances*

Interesting, informative and entertaining,
each Harlequin Romance portrays an appealing
and original love story. With a varied array
of settings, we may lure you on an African safari,
to a quaint Welsh village, or an exotic Riviera
location—anywhere and everywhere that adventurous
men and women fall in love.

As publishers of Harlequin Romances, we're
extremely proud of our books. Since 1949,
Harlequin Enterprises has built its publishing
reputation on the solid base of quality and
originality. Our stories are the most popular
paperback romances sold in North America; every
month, six new titles are released and sold at
nearly every book-selling store in Canada and the
United States.

For a list of all titles currently available,
send your name and address to:

HARLEQUIN READER SERVICE,
(In the U.S.) P.O. Box 52040, Phoenix, AZ 85072-2040
(In Canada) P.O. Box 2800, Postal Station A
5170 Yonge Street, Willowdale, Ont. M2N 6J3

We sincerely hope you enjoy reading
this Harlequin Romance.

Yours truly,

THE PUBLISHERS
Harlequin Romances

Silent Stream

Rowan Kirby

Harlequin Books

TORONTO • NEW YORK • LONDON
AMSTERDAM • PARIS • SYDNEY • HAMBURG
STOCKHOLM • ATHENS • TOKYO • MILAN

Original hardcover edition published in 1984
by Mills & Boon Limited

ISBN 0-373-02675-7

Harlequin Romance first edition February 1985

Passions are likened best to floods and streams:
The shallow murmur, but the deep are dumb.
Sir Walter Raleigh, *The Silent Lover*

For
my brother Laurie,
(a Transatlantic Connection)

Copyright © 1984 by Rowan Kirby.
Philippine copyright 1984. Australian copyright 1984.
All rights reserved. Except for use in any review, the reproduction or utilization
of this work in whole or in part in any form by any electronic, mechanical
or other means, now known or hereafter invented, including xerography,
photocopying and recording, or in any information storage or retrieval system,
is forbidden without the permission of the publisher, Harlequin Enterprises
Limited, 225 Duncan Mill Road, Don Mills, Ontario, Canada M3B 3K9. All the
characters in this book have no existence outside the imagination of the
author and have no relation whatsoever to anyone bearing the same name
or names. They are not even distantly inspired by any individual known
or unknown to the author, and all the incidents are pure invention.

The Harlequin trademarks, consisting of the words HARLEQUIN ROMANCE
and the portrayal of a Harlequin, are trademarks of Harlequin Enterprises
Limited; the portrayal of a Harlequin is registered in the United States Patent
and Trademark Office and in the Canada Trade Marks Office.

Printed in U.S.A.

CHAPTER ONE

'WHAT do *you* think, Dr Hope?'

Professor Slocombe—Head of the English Department, Dean of the Faculty of Arts at this dignified seat of learning—regarded his lecturer in Mediaeval Literature over the top of his bifocals. Then he linked his bony fingers and leaned back in his chair at the head of the long table, allowing his dry glance to encompass the rest of the assembled company.

Dr Hope had not, regrettably, been concentrating on the matter in hand. Her mind, usually so alert, had been wandering among problems of a more domestic nature. She had focussed her warm brown gaze carefully on to a point straight ahead, adopting her most studious expression while pros and cons of whatever vital issue it might be hurled themselves across the table around her.

Dr Hope's neighbour, an intelligent young woman with a round face and short, light-brown hair, gave her a surreptitious but hefty nudge in the ribs. 'Tess! You're being consulted!' she hissed out of the corner of her mouth.

Without batting an eyelid, Dr Hope removed her reading glasses and thoughtfully chewed the end of one earpiece. Then, slowly and deliberately, she turned to the Chairman of the termly Faculty meeting, still waiting patiently for her opinion at the far end of the table, and treated him to one of her broadest grins. Her shrewd eyes lit up in its glow; she ran a firm hand through her luxuriant dark curls, tilting her fine head to one side as she reflected on his question.

Only, of course, she hadn't heard his question. Not that a little thing like that would disconcert Dr Tess Hope. 'Well,' she began on a pensive note, weighing it up carefully, 'it all depends.'

'Depends upon what, Dr Hope?' The eminent Professor was quite used to the habits of his fellow academics: the waffling, the fence-sitting that went on at all such gatherings. Mind you, young Dr Hope was usually less prone to such vagueness than most; but we all have our off-days. 'Can you be more specific?'

'It depends,' she explained confidently, 'on which way you look at it. I mean . . .'

Her neighbour spotted an opportunity to step in and rescue her. 'What Dr Hope is thinking, surely,' she suggested, 'is that the students themselves might have strong feelings on this subject. After all, they'd be as much affected as anyone by this proposal to amalgamate the historical and literary aspects of the Mediaeval Studies syllabus as part of a General Arts degree.'

'Thank you, Mrs Raines.' Tess Hope flashed a barely-perceptible spark of gratitude at her friend and colleague. 'That's just what I had in mind. Their views are supposed to be represented,' she pointed out, as if she had been mulling this precise problem over all along. 'They won't be very pleased if they discover we've made such a major policy decision without consulting them. You know how vociferous students can be,' she reminded them sweetly.

'Given half a chance,' muttered an irascible voice from among the elderly, donnish element opposite her. She recognised it as belonging to the Senior Reader in Anglo-Saxon and Old Norse.

'There's no question of making policy decisions at this stage,' the Chairman was repeating laboriously. 'This is merely a tentative proposal which I am putting before the Meeting for its provisional consideration.'

Tess inclined her head graciously. 'Of course,' she acknowledged. 'Well, my first reaction is not particularly favourable,' she admitted, putting her glasses on again to glance knowledgeably at her notes. 'But I'll give it some thought,' she promised, beaming once again in the direction of the Dean.

'Please do that, Dr Hope. After all, you would be as much involved in such a change as anyone—at present you have sole responsibility for the literary side of the Mediaeval course, and little to do with the History Department. If this were to be implemented, you would have to work much more closely with our friends along the corridor.'

'I appreciate that,' Tess agreed gravely. She toyed with the idea of asking what the Historians themselves thought about the idea, but decided against it, since they had probably been holding forth at some length on that very theme while her mind had been busily engaged a very long way away. She'd have to check it out with Hilary afterwards. Thank God she could be relied on to take things in. Times like this, you really knew who your friends were.

'Very well, then,' Professor Slocombe said with the faintest trace of a bone-dry smile. Then he cleared his throat—a sound like crackling parchment—and turned his watery gaze back to the agenda. 'Shall we proceed with item number twelve on your list, ladies and gentlemen—Any Other Business?'

The rest of the meeting followed its usual dull routine. Tess kept half an ear on what was said, but her thoughts were now running on the proposal she had just been so unexpectedly faced with. Amalgamate two separate courses into one? What a cheek! The more she thought about it, the more indignant she felt. She had built up that Mediaeval Literature course almost single-handed, ever since it had been incorporated into the General Arts degree. She had held sway in her little niche, bringing the Middle Ages to life for her students, studying Chaucer and his contemporaries—not only their writing and the language, but also their lives and the times they lived in. As far as she was concerned, it was an English course. She'd fought long and hard to establish it, worked determinedly to get it the way she wanted it. She enjoyed it, and so did the students—their results were excellent. There seemed no point in interfering with it. They did History under the History slot in the curriculum, and that department could do what it liked; but it could leave her courses alone.

At last the agenda ground to its conclusion, and there was a general shuffling of papers and buzz of conversation. Tess yawned, stretched and looked at her watch. 'Two hours! They get longer and longer.'

Her neighbour laughed. 'You don't usually have such trouble keeping up with our illustrious colleagues, Dr Hope. What's on your mind?'

Tess grinned ruefully. 'You're right, Hil. I'm grateful to you for bailing me out just now. It was brilliantly done—a master-stroke of diplomacy. I have to admit that I hadn't heard a word for at least five minutes.'

'*Is* something on your mind?' pressed her friend.

'As a matter of fact, yes.'

'Personal? Intellectual? Health? The state of the economy? Split ends?'

'None of those. It's my property-owner's hat I'm wearing this time. Bricks and mortar. Realities.'

'The house?' Hilary raised her delicate brows. 'What's wrong?' Tess's little house—two up, two down, a Victorian terraced cottage in a quiet road in North London—was her pride and joy. She owned it herself; or rather, she held the substantial mortgage on it with a local building society. It represented her security, as well as her fiercely-guarded independence, all rolled into one: the two most important things, Hilary Raines knew, in this single working girl's life.

'The cellar,' Tess told her gloomily, her brown eyes troubled. 'Last night I went down there to find an old suitcase for someone to borrow. I hadn't been down for—I don't know—a few days, perhaps. Last time I went it was perfectly all right. Last night it was wet through.'

'Wet?' Hilary frowned. 'How wet?'

'Decidedly wet. Flooded, you might say—the floor was covered. I had to take everything out. I had some old clothes in a trunk, and the water had got in and they were completely soggy. So was the trunk. One old coat had started to grow mould.' She sighed. 'It used to be such a dry cellar—the surveyor who looked at the house particularly remarked on it. It's very peculiar.'

'What did you do? Was anything leaking?' Hilary eyed Tess sympathetically, wondering what she herself would have done. Tim was always there to take over in such emergencies—not that she couldn't have coped alone, of course—just that he was there, and he tended to be the one who dealt with these things. Now, if it had been anything to do with one of the children . . .

'What could I do?' Tess shrugged. 'I mopped up as much as I could, turned off the mains, hoped it wouldn't rise too far in the night.'

'And did it?'

'I was down there first thing this morning. It had risen another half-inch or so, I swear. There's water, water everywhere—great pools of it, about an inch deep in places. I rang the Water Board as soon as they opened, and they said they'd send someone round this afternoon.' She glanced at her watch again. 'I must run, Hil. I said I'd be there by four-thirty, and it's almost four now.'

'Pity—I was about to ask you to have tea. But obviously you must get back. What a strange thing!' Hilary thought about it, puzzled. 'I can't think what might cause it. You must have a burst pipe or something. But don't worry, Tess—I'm sure it won't be anything dire.'

'I sincerely hope not,' Tess said grimly. She stacked her papers together between slim hands that sported an unusual assortment of rings worn on unusual fingers. Then she stood up—a moderately tall, well-built young woman, as striking in form as in feature with her generous figure, dark colouring, lively expression and full, humorous mouth. She was wearing stylish baggy cord slacks which tapered to narrow cuffs over short leather boots, a soft grey shirt and a brightly-striped, hand-knitted sleeveless pullover.

Hilary stood too. 'Don't worry,' she said again. 'These things always seem more dramatic than they are.'

'As long as it doesn't seem more expensive than it is,' replied Tess sardonically. 'I'll let you know how it goes. 'Bye, Hil; and thanks again,' she added as an afterthought, before turning to walk quickly away.

'Don't be silly—you'd do the same for me,' Hilary called after her with a smile. 'See you tomorrow!'

Tess hurried along to her room to collect her coat and briefcase, then set off down the corridor to the lift. As the doors closed, the breathless form of one of the young postgraduate students tumbled in. He collapsed against the wall as the old machine creaked its way downwards. 'Whew! Just in time!' he gasped.

She grinned at him. 'Hallo, Mike. Didn't see you at the Faculty meeting?'

'No way. Got no time for those affairs . . . bore the

pants off me.' He was big and stocky, with untidy fair hair. 'I suppose they told you about this American big noise who's due over here any day now?' Getting his breath back, he regarded her with interest.

'I don't think anything was said about such a person . . . but I wasn't listening to absolutely every word,' Tess admitted cautiously.

'Wicked lady,' he reproached her. 'And you're the one everyone else usually runs to for the latest bulletins—you or Hilary Raines. You must be losing your grip, Doc Hope.'

'I must be,' she agreed mildly.

'Well, I'm surprised they didn't mention this guy, or even introduce him, because he's supposed to be supervising the combining of some courses, and one of them is yours. It's his speciality—Mediaeval Studies—that's partly why he's been invited.'

Tess pricked up her ears. 'Oh yes?' So this business had gone further and deeper than the good Professor had been letting on. 'How did you know all this?'

'I've got inside information from a mole on the History front, don't forget.' She remembered that Mike was going out with a junior lecturer in that department. 'You know their prof—Jim Hewison—has just gone to Canada for a sabbatical?'

'Now that you mention it, I do recall something of the sort.' The internal affairs of the History Department were of little interest to her. 'What of it?'

'They've got this bright spark along to replace him—a certain Professor Joshua Mayer from Princeton, USA. Something of a big deal, it seems, in his field—author of a whole brace of successful publications, well-known whizz-kid of the academic scene over there.'

'And what might his . . . field be?' she enquired coldly as the lift bumped gently at ground-floor level.

'He's a social historian, I understand. Graciously allocating us a few months of his precious time, in order to pursue researches for his latest work—which apparently concerns London.'

'How nice for the History Department,' Tess observed as she walked out of the lift. Mike hurried to catch up with her brisk pace.

'Nice for you too, Dr Hope,' he teased, 'since you'll be working at close quarters. If your course is combined with his, he'll be more or less in charge of it. Your autonomy is under threat, Tess,' he warned irritatingly.

'We'll have to see about that,' Tess flung over her shoulder. Then she was out of the building, running across the wide courtyard and out into the street. Ten minutes later she was on top of a bus carving its cumbersome way northwards. Time enough later to sort out any little problems presented by unwelcome intruders from across the Atlantic into her well-regulated working life. Just now she had more pressing things on her mind.

It was only October, but the sun was already low in the autumnal sky as she walked the half-mile from the bus stop to her street. It seemed curiously depressing to remember that only a matter of weeks ago she had been basking in the Normandy sunshine with her oldest school friend, Anne. And now it was two months to Christmas, and the term was well under way. The long vacation—it stretched away endlessly when viewed from the beginning, during those wonderfully elastic June days; then suddenly it was over, and the new year was upon them again, with its new students—who looked younger every year, Tess reflected—and its interminable committee meetings and its rearranged courses . . .

Her pace always quickened as she approached the little house, smart with cream paint and green door, cheerful with windowboxes and orange curtains. She was deeply proud of it; and not only that—she loved it, as one loves a friend. She didn't want it to suffer from ailments—cracks, or rot, or rising damp. Rising damp! That was a good one: more like pouring wet. She wondered whether her insurance covered her for flood as well as fire. Acts of God, she thought cynically—that was probably it; she was being punished for some inadvertent misdemeanour. It had to be inadvertent: she couldn't recall any serious enough to merit such retribution.

There was no sign of a Water Board van parked outside, no lurking official on the doorstep. Good—she had arrived first; she would have felt at a disadvantage, coming home to find them waiting, and she didn't like feeling at a disadvantage. This would give her time to go down there and inspect the latest damage; maybe even grab a much-needed cup of tea.

She scrabbled in her shoulder-bag for her key-ring. She remembered when the first keys to her first proper home had been cut, the day she moved in. It had been such a momentous occasion in her life: the culmination of all her ideals of self-reliance; a true mark of her successfully independent status. She had had independence drilled into her from her earliest days. Born nearly twenty-eight years ago to a professional couple who had considered themselves well beyond the stage of childrearing—well set into their peaceful, ordered, childless routine—she had been simultaneously adored and neglected. Her father, an eminent research scientist, had been well into his fifties; her mother, a respected artist, was the wrong side of forty. There had been no sign of babies in the twenty years of their placid marriage, so when Tess decided to arrive, the shock was considerable.

'It does happen sometimes,' the family doctor had

explained to them. 'The body has a last fling before
leaving all that side of things behind for ever. Most
people regard it as a bonus—an unexpected blessing.'

Tess's parents had done their best to regard her as a
bonus. As blessings go, she was certainly unexpected. If
she had put in an appearance fifteen, even ten years
earlier, she would have been greeted with open arms and
cries of joy. As it was . . . there was no doubting their
devotion, but the little girl had to fit in with her parents'
long-established patterns of experience rather than the
other way round. She grew up learning to amuse herself,
make few demands—physical or emotional—and do
things her own way before bothering them. She had
everything she needed—even the affection was there if
she went out of her way to ask for it—but it was an
unnaturally aloof, calm, clockwork environment that
prevailed in the handsome Hampstead house, never
changing as the years rolled by.

By the time Tess had left university and gone on to
write her thesis, her father was a very old man; and soon
after she achieved her Ph.D., he died. Her mother, far
from young herself, had sold up the house and moved to
the coast to join her younger sister in sheltered accom-
modation. They were still there: two elderly ladies
together in a small flat, cared for in emergency but
otherwise stubbornly independent, as they had been
taught to be, in their turn, many years ago. The family
had a long history of treating its women as equals,
educating them to a high standard, expecting at least as
good a performance in life from them as from its men.
Tess had inherited this tradition, and was deeply conscious of it.

She went down to visit her mother and aunt sometimes, even though it seemed to be all the same to them
whether she was there or not. They never wanted to

know anything about her life, personal or professional. They would all sit round with cups of china tea in the neat sitting room, discussing some objective topic of news in desultory tones; and Tess was always glad to get home again. She was fond enough of her mother, but there seemed absolutely nothing she could do for her; she still lived in a world which might never have included a daughter.

Moving out of the family home, Tess had shared flats with various friends from school and college, but she had always longed for a place of her own. At last, three years ago, she had achieved her ambition: a permanent post on the staff of the English Department of one of London University's oldest colleges; and soon after that, the purchase of her own small piece of London. Her own roof, her own walls, her own floors, her own space. It was the most important thing in the world to her; and she had lived there alone and contented ever since.

Well, not quite alone. As she let herself into the narrow hall, she was greeted effusively by the other inhabitant of the house. Ginger in complexion and lazy in disposition, he made the perfect foil for his lively dark mistress. He wound himself round her feet now, treating her to a series of non-stop remarks about the fact that she had been gone far too long, and it was time for his tea, and he wouldn't mind stretching his legs in the garden (which was only the size of a postage stamp, but he felt free to expand his territory to include all the neighbouring plots as well); and, while he had her attention, why was there an odd smell of water coming up from the cellar? Was she having a campaign to drown out his mice?

Tess dumped her bag and coat on a chair and stooped to pick him up. He switched on a purr that throbbed right through her. She hugged him, glad of the warmth of his body and his welcome. He was always there to be relied on, whatever the human race and the rest of life threw in her face. She loved her cat, from his splendid whiskers to his white paws, almost as much as she loved her house.

'What's eating you?' she wondered, putting him down and stroking his sleek fur. 'Or have I hit on the problem—did I forget to feed you this morning?' He replied mournfully that she had. 'Poor starved thing! I had a lot on my mind. Oh, Fritz!' She buried her face in her hands, overcome briefly by life's complications. 'Don't let it be anything . . . serious. Just when I've got this place all sorted out the way I want it. Above all, don't let it be anything expensive.' Fritz continued to show more interest in his empty bowl, so she sighed, stood up, filled the kettle and put it on the gas, then attended to her pet's gastronomic needs. He attacked the food with all the gusto of a well-fed animal pretending to be fading away, and she watched him fondly as she sipped her comforting mug of tea.

'Tea,' she observed to his waving tail. 'What would we do without it?' Busy with his bowl, Fritz had nothing to offer on that subject.

The doorbell galvanised her into action, and she slammed the mug down on the small pine table. 'Damn! I haven't even looked to see what's going on down there.' Too late now, she realised: whatever had happened since this morning, it would have to be inspected in the presence of the Water Board representative. She went to open the front door.

He was short, smart and very young—younger than Tess by a good couple of years. She looked at him doubtfully. Her opinion of the male sex was not high at the best of times, and this example of the species did not inspire her with confidence. However, if this was his job, she would have to give him a chance, at least. She was nothing if not fair; you couldn't accuse Tess Hope of prejudice—except, of course, against chauvinist men.

'Good afternoon,' he began politely. His voice was thin and rather high. 'Miss Hope?'

'Dr Hope, yes,' she amended, fixing him with her steady gaze. Not that her academic distinctions mattered to her that much; but it seemed important to take any opportunity to remind members of the opposite gender that females could compete with them successfully in this respect as in every other. 'You must be the man from . . .'

'Thames Water—yes, madam.' She warmed to him. Madam, rather than miss, was a step in the right direction, even if it did make her feel ninety-two. But you couldn't win, she knew; if he had called her 'miss', she would have felt insulted. 'I believe you are having some trouble with rising damp?'

'It's a bit more than rising damp,' she informed him. 'Come in.'

He came in. She remembered that she should have asked for his credentials; but his Water Board van was parked at the curb and she was sure he must be *bona fide*. After all, who else knew about her flood? 'Cup of tea?' she offered kindly. 'I've only just made it.'

'No, thank you, madam. I had one at my last port of call.'

'Right. Well, shall we inspect the site?' she suggested briskly.

'If we might.' He was all starchy correctness: most irritating, she thought. Still, at least he wasn't one of those men with eyes that bored through you, imparting insolent messages even as their lips spoke the formalities. She didn't know which she despised most: men who treated women as sex objects, or those who

behaved as if they were no different from themselves.
It was a dilemma which had confused her for years. She
suspected there must be a happy medium somewhere,
but she had never found it; consequently she avoided all
but necessary professional contact with men, refusing
most of the many offers of their company which she
regularly received.

She didn't miss their company. She preferred her own
in any case—and Fritz's, of course. If she was missing
out on anything, she wasn't aware of it. Her brief sexual
encounters had been superficial and unsatisfactory; and
as for love—well, she suspected it of being a convenient
invention of the media to inveigle women into a life of
dependent drudgery. What was it the posters said . . .
'You start by sinking into his arms, and end up with your
arms in his sink.' It was a warning she could not afford to
ignore.

This particular young man looked as though he
wouldn't recognise an insolent message if one landed on
him. Switching on the cellar light, she led him down the
steep stairs. Stopping at the bottom, they both looked
round. The water was still at the level she had seen it at
last night. Apparently it was not about to swamp the
whole house; that was something.

'Hmmm,' he remarked. Tess looked at him anxiously;
they had such power, people who were experts in things
you knew nothing about. She had always hated being in
their hands. 'Hmmm,' he repeated, even more meaningfully.

'Hmmm?' she echoed.

'Not a large cellar, is it, madam,' he observed helpfully. 'More of a coalhole really. Have you ever used it
for coal?'

'No.' She gave him a withering look. 'I have gas
central heating.'

He was undaunted. 'But is there a vent at the front of the house where they used to pour the coal through? Sometimes, when it rains heavily, water can get in through those and settle on a cellar floor . . .'

'It hasn't been raining heavily,' she pointed out, 'and I've never noticed it doing that, even when it did.'

'No.' He bent down and measured the depth of the water with one finger. Then he tapped a few pipes in an ineffectual sort of way. 'Any burst pipes? Have you tried turning it off at the mains?'

'The first thing I did was to turn the stopcock off, but it didn't make any difference. I was hoping you'd be able to tell *me* if I had a burst pipe.'

'That's more of a job for a plumber,' he told her in his flat tones. 'But I'd say, at a cursory glance, that you haven't.'

'Then what, at a cursory glance, would you say I *have* got?' She was losing the private struggle to keep the sarcasm out of her voice.

But it was lost on him. He continued to stare down at the brown water that lowered at them from the floor. 'Have you noticed it's moving?' he asked suddenly.

'Moving?' She looked more closely at it. Yes, he was right—it was flowing through the cellar. A sluggish, murky trickle, but undoubtedly moving. 'So it is.' She almost gave way to panic. 'What does that mean?'

He shrugged. 'Not a lot. If the house is on any sort of slope, I suppose it would flow downhill. Are you sure you've never noticed it before?' he persisted.

'Never. It's been as dry as a bone down here. I store things here—well, I did, up to now,' she added sadly.

'Hmmm,' he said again, more annoyingly than ever. 'I think I'll have to get advice on this—look into this area as a whole, see if any main drains have been disturbed or become blocked in the vicinity. Sometimes we get reports of this happening in several places at once, then we have to look into the overall cause,' he explained pompously.

'Yes, you would have to.' Her tone was wry. 'And what do you find?'

He turned to face her for the first time. His light blue eyes rested on her face with surprising directness. Perhaps he wasn't so pathetic after all; she felt unaccountably ashamed. 'It depends. It has been known to be due to the flooding of a river.'

Her dark eyebrows lifted into her curls. 'A river? But I'm nowhere near . . .'

'Nearer than you think. I mean an underground river. There are plenty of those about, as I'm sure you know.'

'Oh yes,' she agreed carelessly, though she had never heard of any such thing.

'Well, sometimes they don't want to stay underground and they come up through whatever gets in their way— houses, roads—and this is what happens.'

'Do they go down again?'

'As often as not. But it may not be that,' he reminded her. 'I'll have it carefully investigated. Meanwhile, it's not doing too much harm, as long as it stays at this level. If it rises any further, let us know at once. Otherwise we'll be in touch with you again, Miss Hope, as soon as we've completed our local search.'

'Dr Hope,' she corrected automatically as she led the way back up the stairs. 'So there's nothing you can do at the moment?'

'Nothing, I'm afraid.' She opened the front door to see him out. 'But don't worry, madam,' he told her kindly. 'We'll soon have you sorted out. We're used to all kinds of dramatic situations. Sometimes,' he added reassuringly, 'people's whole downstairs fills up like a swimming pool.'

Tess watched as he closed the gate carefully behind him and fitted his dapper frame behind the wheel of the Water Board van. 'Thanks a million!' she muttered, as its rear lights disappeared down the darkening street.

CHAPTER TWO

'WHAT on earth do you mean—a river?' Hilary, standing next to Tess in the queue for lunch in the college cafeteria, turned to face her, registering surprise.

'I mean exactly that. That's what the young person said. A river, under the ground, that bursts its banks and floods cellars. I had a good look after he went, but I couldn't see any silver trout or gleaming pebbles or fronds of weed. Not even an old anchor rusting away at the bottom of the stream. It just looks like a trickle of sludge; but that's what he said.' Tess sighed heavily. 'Trust me to pick a house that was built on top of a river! What was it doing there in the first place, I'd like to know?'

The queue moved forward a few inches towards the overpowering aroma of fried onion, sausages and canteen coffee. 'It's an amazing thought,' Hilary said. 'More exciting than a burst pipe, don't you think?'

'More exciting, perhaps,' Tess agreed lugubriously. 'But infinitely more alarming.' For the umpteenth time since the previous evening, her mind let itself wander disconcertingly over the possibilities. The water would eat away into her foundations, she was sure—rotting her wood, powdering her brick, crumbling her stone, until the whole house just keeled over . . .

'It doesn't need to be alarming.' A male voice—very male indeed—offered this philosophical comment from immediately behind them, and they both swung round to investigate the uninvited intrusion into their conversation.

It was a mark of how engrossed they had been that they had not noticed him before. He towered head and shoulders above most of the rest of the queue; and they were not just any old head and shoulders. The head was endowed with a thick, vital mane—its springing blackness thrown into sharp relief by an occasional white streak, a greying at the temples. The shoulders were broad, powerful; the whole frame, clothed casually in close-fitting denim, jeans and navy sweatshirt, shouted of contained vigour and strength. The voice that had interrupted them was rich and deep, its inflections not quite English but not instantly identifiable.

Grinning under their frank scrutiny, he spoke again. 'Forgive me for eavesdropping, young ladies, but I have come across this phenomenon before. It's not uncommon—there's no need to worry about it.'

Young ladies! They exchanged glances: very few people around here addressed anyone as 'young ladies', even in that slightly ironic tone. Tess, as usual, was uncertain whether to feel pleased or insulted. She looked directly up into his face, and wished she hadn't. She had never seen a face like it; its effect was magnetic. Swarthy skin went with the black hair, but the eyes were a cool, astonishing grey—deep and faintly mottled, like ancient stone—their expression a battleground between humour and intensity. The mouth, long and deeply-carved, shared the same conflict: there was the wry twist at one corner, the sensitive, sensuous thrust of the lower lip. The nose was hooked—positive, forceful, an eagle's beak; the chin square, determined. They were features which screamed their potency at you; not the kind you went away and forgot.

And Tess was standing next to them. She cleared her throat, aware that the grey eyes were scanning her own face and body without embarrassment or compunction.

It was up to her to say something; Hilary was rooted to the spot, the other side of her, like a bump on a log—it was no use expecting help from her this time. 'Oh yes?' she ventured, her voice only slightly lower than its usual firm self.

He had thick dark eyebrows which habitually knitted together, giving him a half puzzled, half sardonic appearance. 'In the course of years of research,' he expanded, 'I've come to recognise certain patterns. Such subterranean streams are a direct reflection of the development of the cities they flow through. They were usually forced underground by those who were responsible for that development.'

Tess supposed this made some sort of sense, but she was finding it difficult to take words in at all through the impact of his physical presence. The queue jostled forward again. 'I see.' She looked away, then looked up at him again; he was still regarding her quizzically. Involuntarily, she moved away from his overpowering influence—treading on Hilary's toe in the process.

'Ouch!' Hilary squeaked.

'Sorry,' Tess muttered.

Hilary managed a grin. 'That's okay. Look, it's our turn. Come on—what are you having?'

Tess forced her attention reluctantly to the unappetising spread before them. 'Cheese salad, I think, a roll, and tea.' She smiled at the woman behind the counter. 'Hallo, Joan. How're things?'

'Mustn't grumble,' the woman replied, grumbling. 'What about you?'

'I'm fine—except I've got a river running through my house.'

'Running through your house? Good lord, whatever next?' Joan exclaimed conversationally. She giggled. 'Now, that's what I call an unusual feature.'

'I'm thinking of letting the fishing rights,' Tess announced matter-of-factly. Joan giggled again, and so did Hilary.

'May I enquire,' their neighbour cut in, helping himself to a plate of cold ham and salad, 'whether it's actually running *through* your house? In the literal sense of the word?'

Tess got some money out of her purse as they reached the checkout. 'Yes, I suppose you could say it is.'

'Look, I'm really interested in this.' Tess was intrigued, in spite of herself, by his accent. There was Canadian or American there—and other things as well. 'Could I join you ladies for lunch, and maybe you could tell me more about this . . . river?'

They paid, and stood clutching their trays, eyeing each other doubtfully. It wasn't every day a complete stranger invited himself to have lunch with them—least of all one like this. The college didn't go in for exciting new people. Tess was unimpressed, naturally; but she could see that Hilary, despite her happily married status, was bowled over. To humour her, she decided to agree. 'Why not, eh, Hil?'

'I don't mind.' Hilary risked a glance at their new acquaintance, who grinned disarmingly back.

'That's surely good of you, ladies,' he drawled—with unnecessary emphasis, in Tess's opinion. Not even an American needed to be *that* American. Not that she had anything against Americans. They could be rather . . . brash; but never let it be said that she held irrational preconceptions about anyone—their sex, race or class.

They sat down at a corner table and unloaded their trays. Hilary, unable to meet their companion's gaze, stared instead at her pie and chips. 'Why don't I have salad like you? I'm always going to, but somehow I always get greedy at the last moment.'

'Now then.' Their new friend settled his large frame as comfortably as possible on a spindly canteen chair. Tess tried not to notice the way his hands were strong but strangely delicate, the fingers long and elegant as they picked up the knife and fork. 'Tell me more.'

'Not much more to tell,' said Tess, taking a mouthful of salad. 'I woke up one morning to find water flowing through my cellar. Next thing I know, I'm being told it might be a river. All I can say is, I wish it had chosen some other person's property to surface in. I was quite happy about my little house till this happened.'

The grey eyes regarded her steadily. 'It could be a very good sign. Rivers have good vibes, you know—they choose their path carefully. Had you thought about that? Your house might have been built at a lucky spot.'

She returned his gaze scornfully. She had no time for such whimsical fancies. 'As far as I'm concerned,' she retorted, 'it's nothing but a nuisance.'

'What's your interest?' Hilary was genuinely fascinated by this stranger—in more ways than one. 'Is it your line of work?'

'It sure is. I'm a social historian. I have a special interest in the way big cities grew up around little villages—the way the countryside is still there underneath the concrete and brick. I've dealt with this theme in a number of my books about different places . . . and I'm partly here to look into it in London.'

A warning light flicked on in Tess's brain. There was something familiar here: she knew who this man was. There couldn't be two social historians here at the college whom they'd never seen before . . . and Americans at that . . . but she wouldn't say anything until she'd checked her hunch out. For the moment she let him go on talking, but watched him carefully from under lowered lashes.

'Where do you live?' he was asking eagerly now. Since the question was obviously of professional interest only, she thought she might as well answer it—wary as she normally was to guard her privacy. 'On the borders of Tufnell Park and Highgate. Mean anything to you?'

'It most certainly does!' There was a gleam of excitement now in the grey eyes. 'This isn't my first visit to London, by any means. Quite apart from its being a pleasant area to live in, that's just where one of these rivers does run,' he told her, his tone warm with enthusiasm.

'Oh yes?' Steeling herself against that mesmerising gaze, she looked at him again. 'Which one?'

'It's called the Fleet. I can tell you any amount of fascinating things about that waterway. I have maps and notebooks and textbooks full of references to its course and its history. It wasn't always underground; in fact it's only been pushed under very recently—less than two hundred years. Before that it was a perfectly ordinary river, running right through the centre of London.'

'I've heard of it, of course,' Tess admitted.

'Presumably Fleet Street was named after it,' Hilary suggested. 'And didn't there used to be a Fleet Prison?'

'There certainly did.' He was warming to his theme now, waving those expressive hands for emphasis as he talked. 'And not too far from where you live. Miss . . .' he turned to Tess, 'there's a Fleet Road, if I'm not very much mistaken?'

Tess deliberately failed to rise to his bait and tell him her name. 'No, it's not so far from where I live. But it's nearer to where my friend here lives—isn't it, Hil?'

'That's right—on the way to Hampstead. Gospel Oak, that's where I live.'

'Well, the Fleet flows right along there. Perhaps you

both live on its banks, if you did but know it,' he announced triumphantly.

They were silent for a few moments, digesting the possibility of such an unlikely fact in the middle of one of the oldest, greatest cities in the world. Hilary speared a chip with her fork. 'It's hard to believe,' she mused.

'Very,' Tess agreed cynically.

'You'd better believe it, ladies,' he assured them solemnly. There was a short pause. 'I can't go on calling you "ladies",' he complained. 'May I be so bold as to enquire your names?'

'I'm Hilary Raines,' Hilary told him.

'Glad to know you, Mrs Raines.' He reached a firm hand across the table to shake hers. Tess stifled a grin at the expression on Hilary's face—he had noticed her wedding ring, and her look of pride mingled with disappointment was positively comic. 'And what do I call you?' he asked, turning to her abruptly.

'My name is Hope,' she told him stiffly.

The eyebrows shot up. 'Now, that's a new one on me. I've known a couple of Faiths, even a Charity, but never a Hope. Are you as optimistic as your name suggests?' he mocked gently.

'Hope is my surname,' she explained, irritated. 'My first name is Tess.'

'Tess.' He tried it out on his tongue, and seemed to approve. 'Tess—that's nice. It suits you. Is it short for anything? Teresa? Tessa?'

'No. My parents were keen on Thomas Hardy,' she told him unwillingly, wishing he would mind his own business.

'Ah yes, the lovely Tess of the D'Urbervilles. Haven't we all been in love with her at some time in our foolish youth?' He smiled, and she looked away again. That smile did things she disliked intensely to her stomach,

tightening her chest into a tense lump. She wished he
would keep his hooked nose out of her affairs; but it was
too late now. 'It's a lovely name, Miss Hope,' he added
graciously.

She ignored the arch compliment. '*Dr* Hope,' she
amended, poker-faced.

'Dr Hope?' He frowned. 'Now where have I heard
that name before . . .' He stared at her speculatively.
'You don't work in the English Department, by any
chance, do you?'

She nodded. 'That's me.' He was getting the message;
light was dawning.

'Mediaeval Studies your specialty?'

'The very same.'

'Well now, that sure is a coincidence. Do you know
who I am?'

'I have a fair idea,' she assured him coolly. 'Professor
Mayer? From Princeton University? Honouring the History Department with your presence for a year in the
absence of Jim Hewison?'

Hilary was gazing at her in amazement. 'How did you
know that, Tess?'

'I have my spies. Actually, I was about to tell you,
over lunch. It seems I've been pre-empted by . . . the
man himself.' She glanced across the table at him.

The man himself was now regarding her with even
more direct curiosity. 'Your speculation is quite accu-
rate. I'm Joshua Mayer. I had no idea my fame had
spread before me,' he drawled. 'And there was nothing
in Professor Slocombe's letter,' he continued thoughtfully, his eyes narrowing upon her face, 'to suggest that
Dr Hope was female.'

'Well, I am, as you see,' she pointed out.

'I do indeed,' he acknowledged, his tone wry.

'I'd heard of you anyway,' Hilary blurted out, overwhelmed with admiration. 'Don't you write books? I'm sure Tim's got one by you—about—where was it? Bangkok? Hong Kong?'

'Could be either,' he confessed lightly. 'I've done both.'

'And now,' Tess supplied, 'you've come to "do" London.'

'Correct.' Grey eyes clashed with brown, and her antagonism sharpened as she remembered what his presence might mean to her working arrangements. 'I think,' he went on, the merest suggestion of a smile at the corner of his mouth, 'we're destined to work in harness, Miss—er—Dr Hope. Am I right?'

Not if I have anything to do with it, her mind answered him grimly; but all she said was: 'I had heard something of the kind, Professor Mayer. It hasn't yet been confirmed, as I understand it. Nothing has been officially decided.' Hilary looked from one to the other, quite lost in this conversation. Her eyes implored Tess to explain what was going on. 'I was going to tell you that too, Hil, but once again I appear to have been . . .forestalled.'

'I have only just arrived at your excellent college,' Joshua Mayer informed Hilary in clipped tones. 'But from the basic briefing I'd already received, I gather that there is a course in Mediaeval Studies, at the moment run largely by Dr Hope as part of the General Arts degree.'

'Run entirely by Tess,' amended Hilary loyally, beginning to comprehend the way things might be.

'Up until now, run by Dr Hope,' he conceded blandly. 'But the Faculty have clearly realised there's more scope for a History than an English Department in dealing with such a wide and varied topic. The literature is, after all, only one part of what the students need to know— and a small part, at that,' he added with a glance in Tess's direction. 'There are many other, equally vital, aspects of the period—with which, as a social historian specialising in it, I'm deeply familiar.' There was an arrogance now in his tone, the set of his head, which caused Tess's hackles to rise still further. She might have known! Men like him were all the same—unbearably superior, sure they were right.

'Aspects which I've been careful *not* to leave out of my own course,' she retorted succinctly. 'I've never seen it purely as a literature course. Far from it—we've covered all sorts of social and historical angles as well as reading Chaucer and some of the other . . .'

'All the more reason,' he cut in rudely, 'to involve History staff in it as well. I'm not questioning your academic ability, Dr Hope, or the fact that you have doubtless built up a wonderfully comprehensive picture of the era for your students.' Tess found herself wishing she could wipe the complacent smirk off his powerful face; her fingers itched to slap it. 'Your Faculty merely wondered,' he went on, 'whether more of a balance would be achieved if both departments were equally incorporated. Since the students enjoy the course so much,' he added ingratiatingly, 'and it has been so . . . expertly taught, up to now, why not use some of my specific expertise to make it even better?' He leaned back, obviously satisfied with this piece of transparent diplomacy.

But Tess had no time for such wiles. She was not like the other women who, no doubt, fell at his feet when he used them. 'If my students enjoy the course so much,' she threw back, 'and their results are so . . . satisfactory, then why bother to change it at all? Why not leave it as it is—under the auspices of the English Department?'

He shrugged. 'It seems to me,' he suggested acidly, 'that most people would be pleased to have a little of the responsibility taken from their shoulders. And to have it publicly recognised, at the same time, that their ideas are worthy of being developed by one of the top men in the field, who happens to be around for a while.'

Tess glared at him. Lesser men had flinched under that glare; but Joshua Mayer remained unscathed. Hilary ducked as if she could feel the sparks flying physically. There was no point in interfering, she knew—once Tess got her blood up, nothing and no one would stand in her way. Least of all a man; and this was not a man to be trifled with. Later, Hilary would warn her friend—staid old married lady as she was—of the dangers of sparring with such a man . . . if it wasn't too late by then. Meanwhile, she could only sit and act as silent referee— or perhaps, a corner of her mind suggested, as chaperone?

'I'm not most people,' Tess was pointing out in her most biting tones.

He did not reply at once, apparently summing her up. Then, unexpectedly, he grinned. 'You sure aren't,' he acknowledged. 'I have no wish to come halfway across the world to cross swords with beautiful and intelligent young women.' He was resorting to blatant, sexist flattery now—only making her angrier than ever. 'I can get all that at home, and more. I was hoping you British would be different, with that famous reserve of yours.' He sighed ostentatiously. 'It seems I was wrong.'

'That must be an unusual experience for you—being wrong.' Tess flashed, now thoroughly disliking him— and secretly pleased that her reaction to him in the flesh fitted in so well with the opinion she had formed when she had heard about his visit. 'I don't suppose it happens very often?'

'Not often.' His face was impassive, but there was

humour in his eyes, and that amused quirk turning up one corner of his mouth. She hated him more than ever. Downright rage would have been easier to deal with than this . . . this patronising smugness!

'Now listen,' began Hilary hopefully, 'you hardly know each other, and the college has plans for you to work together. Surely this is a destructive way to start things off? I mean . . .' she faltered, as both faces turned in her direction, '. . . surely you could behave like . . .'

'Like the adults we are? In a mature and professional manner?' His expression was cool now, his eyes hard, his mouth straight. 'Quite right, Mrs Raines.'

'Please call me Hilary,' she invited, trying to get things on to a less formal footing.

'Hilary,' he nodded. 'And please call me Josh—all my friends do. I can't expect such intimacies of Dr Hope, perhaps . . .' he turned back to his seething adversary, 'but at least can we call a truce? Your friend's advice is excellent; we are behaving like a couple of . . . under-graduates. I'm sure we can sort this little problem out. I had no idea, when I was invited, that I was stepping into some kind of . . . feminist hornets' nest.'

'It's nothing of the kind!' Tess flung back angrily. She had been quite prepared to accept Hilary's suggestion, but really, this was too much! 'It's got nothing to do with me being a woman. That's typical of your sort of man—as soon as any woman has an opinion of her own, or a complaint to make, they think it's all down to our hormones or something. It's entirely,' she declared, 'a matter of professional pride.'

'Is that right?' Once again he leaned back, non-chalantly scrutinising her—those deep grey eyes never leaving her indignant face. 'Are you so sure of that, Dr Hope? In my experience, nothing is ever quite that simple, where men and women are concerned.'

'And your experience, no doubt, is as wide as the Atlantic,' she growled.

'Not so far off,' he admitted smoothly. 'I've been around a good deal in the course of a long and chequered career. I don't just teach, you know. I travel, I write, I lecture, I research. I make television documentaries. I mingle with Joe Public—and Josephine Public too,' he added meaningfully. 'You learn a lot when you cover as much ground as I do.' And you, his tone suggested, have been stuck here all your life, teaching exactly the same things to indistinguishable students year after year. 'What's more,' he pointed out, 'I can give you a few years, Dr Hope. Don't forget that. I was always taught to defer to the wisdom of age—even if you succeed in forgetting the difference in gender.' The smile was there again now, playing mockingly round the dark countenance.

'Age?' She regarded him scornfully—a man in his prime, maybe ten years older than herself. 'What's that got to do with anything?'

He cast his eyes down in satirical meekness. 'I just thought maybe I could win you over by appealing to your . . . protective instincts: that intrinsic sensitivity some women have. But never mind, I can see you're determined to make a battle out of it.' Tess snorted; she had never in her life met anyone less in need of protection. He stood up—a long way up, and feeling instantly at a disadvantage, Tess stood up too. 'I have to be getting along,' he explained, coldly polite now. 'I have a seminar at two. I wish you the best of luck with your river, Dr Hope. I regret that the circumstances of our meeting have not been conducive to a further mutual investigation into that fascinating subject. When we meet again— as we undoubtedly will—I shall look forward to your being in a more . . . amenable frame of mind.'

For once, words deserted Tess; she could only stare at him in mute hostility. Undeterred, he bowed slightly towards her and then flashed his wide, stunning grin at Hilary. 'It's been a great pleasure to meet you, Hilary. By the way, what's your line? I never asked.'

'I'm in the English Department too. Shakespeare mostly.'

'Ah, Shakespeare. Now there was a man.' He paused, looking through a high window to where London lay spread below them. 'You British may be hung up, and stuck in the mud, these days, but in those days—wow! You really knew how to live—and to write.'

On this tersely enigmatic note he beamed at Hilary again, turned on his heel and strode off.

They watched until he was out of sight; then Tess sat down again. Hilary studied her friend's outraged face. Tess studied the salt-and-pepper pots on the grey formica-topped table.

At last Hilary broke a pregnant silence. 'Stuck in the mud, he said. Do you think we are, Tess?'

'Of course not.' Tess glared at her almost as fiercely as she had glared at Joshua Mayer. 'Don't listen to a word that inflated man says. You could see what he was like.'

'Yes,' Hilary agreed pensively, 'I could.'

'Well then. He's not worth bothering with . . . an arch-MCP. Forget about him—*I* shall,' she declared. 'I've got much more important things to think about.'

'It was interesting, though, wasn't it—what he was saying about the river? The Fleet? Didn't you think so?' Hilary pushed her gently.

'Was it?' Tess frowned. 'I suppose so, if you're into that sort of thing. My only concern is with it being in my cellar. No,' she decided, 'if I'm forced to come into contact with him again, I can't do anything about it . . . but until I do, I'm going to shut that gentleman out of my mind. Stupid nonsense anyway, all this business about the good vibes where rivers run and all that. Rubbish!'

Hilary's perusal of Tess's face became even more thoughtful; but she knew better than to argue with her friend in this mood. She had a suspicion, though, that it might be easier said than done, shutting Joshua Mayer out of one's mind. And somewhere, lurking in the depths of hers, she knew that Tess shared it.

CHAPTER THREE

THE first thing Tess did when she got home that evening was to go down and check on the latest watery developments. Her private river did not appear to have done anything alarming: as far as she could see, the level had neither risen nor fallen.

The second thing she did was to put the kettle on; and the third thing was to feed Fritz, who was prowling hopefully around, complaining as usual of acute starvation. When she had provided him with a bowlful of food, and herself with a steaming mug, she sat down to relax for the first time all day.

But not for long. Within seconds the telephone was stridently demanding her attention from its place in the hall. Sighing, she went through to answer it, taking her tea with her. Automatically she lifted the receiver and quoted her own number into it.

'Hallo—Tess?'

The dry voice was familiar enough—though not so often at the other end of a phone. 'Professor Slocombe?'

'Indeed it is. How clever of you to guess, my dear.'

His dear! He was certainly turning on such reserves of charm as he could find. Immediately she stiffened, suspicious. He was not normally given to making polite calls to his staff. 'What can I do for you, Professor?'

'Well, Tess . . .' (This friendly use of her first name was somewhat unusual, too, now she came to think of it), 'I was hoping we might have a little chat. If you have a few moments to spare?'

A little chat? One did not have *little chats* with Professor Slocombe: one had tutorials, or lengthy discussions, or private lectures. What was he up to? A paranoid certainty was setting in that it had something to do with the great Professor Mayer. 'I have a few moments,' she admitted cautiously, taking a fortifying sip of tea.

'It's about this business of your course. The General Arts one,' he elucidated, in case she hadn't guessed.

'I thought it might be.'

'I feel that things need . . . clarifying,' he suggested.

'You may be right there,' Tess agreed drily.

'It was never my intention that the proposal should come to your notice in that way—at the Faculty meeting. I had meant to speak to you privately first; but you know how it is—the beginning of term—and such matters always seem to progress so quickly, once they're set in motion . . .'

'They do, don't they,' she remarked blandly.

'Er . . . I gather you've now actually met Professor Mayer?' Tess was satisfied to note that he seemed to be having some difficulty in approaching the subject.

'Yes, we did bump into one another, over lunch in the canteen.'

'He said you already knew about his part in the scheme,' he went on uncomfortably.

'I do have colleagues in the History Department, you know, Professor Slocombe,' she pointed out. 'Give people in this establishment the whiff of a piece of news, and wildfire has nothing on the spread of it!'

'Too true, my dear,' Obviously he was determined to keep on the right side of her. Even her biting sarcasm was not going to produce its customary acerbic reaction. 'I really do regret that you had to find out in that way. As I say, I had no intention . . . I meant to tell you myself— but you disappeared rather swiftly after the meeting, as I recall.'

'I had pressing problems at home,' she told him tersely.

'I'm sorry to hear that.' She was surprised to hear a note of genuine sympathy—almost of warmth—in his voice. 'Anything I can do? Or Mrs Slocombe, perhaps?' he added quickly.

He thinks it might be a problem of a female nature, thought Tess sardonically. 'No, but thank you all the same. What was it you wanted to say about this . . . scheme? Couldn't it wait till tomorrow?' She was very tired. She sat down on the stool next to the telephone and took another sip of tea that was rapidly cooling. Fritz had finished his supper, and came purring round her feet.

'That's just it. Tomorrow there's a staff meeting on this very topic. Just the few of us who are involved— yourself, and young Jones from History—and me, and of course Professor Mayer himself. I was hoping you'd be able to come, so that we can sort things out in an amicable fashion. I understand that you feel a little . . . put out . . .'

'Put out! I built that course up virtually alone, Pro- fessor Slocombe,' Tess reminded him vehemently. 'It's taken me two years, and I've had precious little help. Even if I'd wanted the History Department to join in, I doubt whether they'd have spared the man-hours. And now, suddenly, because there's the chance of a bit of kudos from this big fish they've managed to land in their net for a few months, they see fit to take it over—lock, stock and barrel, as far as I can make out. As if I'd never even covered the social or historical angles of the period at all, when I've made a particular point of . . .'

'I know you have, my dear,' the Professor interrupted soothingly. 'I'm only too aware of what a first-rate job you've done with that course. I was only saying as much to the Academic Board the other day. "Dr Hope has

achieved miracles with that Mediaeval Studies programme," I said to them. "She deserves a little support
and recognition for her work." They agreed with me, and
since Professor Mayer was coming here anyway, and it's
his field, we thought . . .'

'Well, I wish you'd thought of asking me first, that's
all.' Tess was already regretting her lapse into vociferous
indignation. She always intended to remain cool and
dignified, maintain an air of detachment—but somehow
it always came flooding out, all that strong feeling, as if a
dam had broken and she could no longer hold it back.
Calm, icy anger and self-control were not in her nature.
'It wasn't a very pleasant way of finding out. And I can't
see why it's necessary to change it, add to it, reorganise
it, combine it with anything else, or whatever. I enjoy it,
the students enjoy it, the External Examiners approve of
it, the Academic Board appreciates it, so why . . . ?'

'To tell you the truth,' the Dean explained confi-
dentially, 'the Vice-Chancellor mentioned it to me himself. He pointed out that it was highly unusual for such
a syllabus to be run entirely under the auspices of an
English Literature lecturer. Apparently at other colleges . . .'

So that was it—the University authorities had been
getting at him! Bureaucracy had raised its red-tape-
bedecked head, as it so often did. 'Why do we have to
take any notice of other colleges?' she enquired coldly.

'As you know, my dear, I'm not noted for my willing-
ness to . . . tow the line in that respect.' She had to admit
that was true. The Dean of Arts was known for his
tendency to go out on a limb in support of his less
orthodox whims. He was not entirely the conventional
creature he might appear on the surface. 'But I had to
concede that he had a valid point. And when it was
brought to my attention that Professor Mayer was due to

make a visit in any case, in order to pursue some researches for his latest piece of work, and that he would be taking on some lecturing as well . . . I could hardly turn down the opportunity. A man like that, with his reputation, his dynamism—he'd bring so much to our . . . to your already splendid efforts.'

She hadn't thought of it quite like that. All the same, it didn't make it any less of a liberty. She still felt vaguely insulted: she could not say exactly why, but she knew she did. 'You really ought to have consulted me in the first place, Professor Slocombe.'

'I know, I know,' he agreed unhappily. But he was aware that he had gained ground; Tess could tell that from the complacent undertone in the parchment-thin voice. 'I feel very bad about that—please believe me, Tess. If you would consent to attend the meeting tomorrow—at three, in the small seminar room—I shall endeavour to make it up to you. I shall make it clear to our distinguished colleague that your role on the course has been of primary importance and must continue to be so.' There was a short pause. 'So—you will come?' he added hopefully.

'I'll be there,' she promised grimly. Perhaps it would be better to make sure she was around while they rearranged her precious material to suit themselves. She couldn't let it slip from her grasp without a struggle. And anyway, once the wonderful Joshua Mayer had disappeared back to the wilds of Princeton whence he came, it would no doubt be left to her to pick up the pieces and go on as before. She'd give them a good run for their money before letting them touch a paragraph of it, that was for sure.

'Oh, good.' He sounded relieved; and perhaps a little surprised. 'I'm so glad. I'm sure, if we all sit down together like . . .'

'Like mature and intelligent people?' she suggested
ironically. It seemed a very short time since someone
else had made a similar remark. Obviously they shared
the same scriptwriter—an unlikely combination, Professors Slocombe and Mayer, but certainly a well-
balanced duo of opposites.

'Precisely,' he agreed gratefully. 'I knew you'd be
reasonable, Tess. You've always been such a reasonable
person . . .'

. . . for a woman, Tess's mind finished the phrase off
on his behalf; but she forced her tone into its calmest,
most rational pitch before replying. 'Thank you. And
now, if there's nothing else . . . ?'

'No, I won't keep you from your . . . your domestic
affairs. Whatever the difficulty is, I hope it resolves itself
soon,' he said, not unkindly. 'Until tomorrow, then.'

'Three o'clock,' Tess confirmed. 'I'll be there.'

She arrived at the seminar room deliberately early. It
made her feel one jump ahead, being first on the scene;
she hated being late for anything, having to walk in when
everyone else was into their stride. She always made
sure she was at lectures and tutorials before her students
got there—unlike some other lecturers who preferred to
keep their audiences waiting in order to ensure maxi-
mum impact. Despite her hot temper, Tess was a
careful, meticulous person.

On this occasion, although she hardly admitted it to
herself, she was determined to be there before the
History contingent. She might as well start off with as
much of an advantage as possible over the great Professor Mayer. It seemed even more important than
usual, for some reason.

But as soon as she entered the small room she knew
she was too late. He was there already, his potent

presence dominating the confined space, standing at the window; intense grey eyes and heavy brows brooding over the view of streets and buildings that stretched relentlessly away. Hearing the door open, he swung round to confront her. Meeting those eyes, Tess barely took in the rest of him—clad today in a smart, informal suit which emphasised the broad cut of his shoulders; his shirt open at the neck to reveal strong, wiry dark hair.

He looked her up and down—the tan knee-length boots, the wide brown wool skirt, the cream blouse— and his eyebrows knitted together in that gesture she already recognised with a jolt. Perhaps she had taken a little more care than usual in dressing this morning; not that it had anything to do with the fact that she knew she was going to encounter him.

'Ah, Dr Hope, we meet again.'

'Professor Mayer.' She inclined her head slightly in cool greeting.

'I was just admiring your view,' he told her, turning back to the window.

'It's just London. Same as any other big city, I imagine.' She sat down at the opposite end of the table and began taking folders and files out of her bag in a businesslike fashion.

'That's where you're wrong.' Once again the deep gaze was steady on her face. She avoided it, concentrating hard on straightening her papers. 'Every city in the world is different—built up of a thousand different ingredients, put together at different times and in different ways by different people . . .'

'Okay, okay, I get the idea.' She smiled but still did not look directly at him. 'I'm being told off by a historian who specialises in dissecting cities, is that it?'

'Not "told off". I would hardly presume to "tell off" a colleague, Dr Hope; I was merely suggesting that you look at your home town through new eyes—take a fresh glance around you. It's not just a twentieth-century hotch-potch of office blocks and suburbs. It goes back to the Romans, and earlier, as I'm sure you must be aware.'

'I was aware of that, yes, thank you Professor—despite being a humble Literature lecturer.' Tess lifted her dark eyes for the first time, and they locked with his. It was like being on the receiving end of a magnetic force.

'Every individual London village has its own tales to tell—its own separate development as a community. It's the same the world over—that's what makes it so exciting. That's why I choose to study them.' The excitement was plain in his voice—vibrant, warm with it. She was still trying to place the accents which lurked beneath those nasal American vowels, but it wasn't easy, even to a linguist like herself.

'And where do Mediaeval Studies come into all this?' she asked coldly. 'You seem to have strayed a long way from your original field—if that's what it was.'

'It was; and it is. I don't make a rigid distinction between one piece of the past and another,' he told her, equally cool. 'I started off in that specialty and I like to think I'm something of an authority on the subject—hence my presence here now.' And modest with it, Tess's mind interposed. 'But I do not approve of the practice of drawing hard-and-fast lines between disciplines. Our heritage is there to be appreciated by us all. All historical research repays study.'

'End of lecture?' Tess enquired, leaning back in her chair and clasping her hands behind her curly dark head.

He grinned; and it illuminated the powerful features, lightening their fierce expression. 'Sorry. I guess I do like to ride my hobbyhorse a bit too hard. I was forgetting that the hidden origins of London are not your favourite topic at the moment.'

Tess raised puzzled eyebrows. 'How do you mean?'

'Your river? The ancient God-made waterway bubbling up through the modern man-made clay? Is it still gracing your cellar?' He left the window and sat down in the chair next to her, causing her pulserate to accelerate to a speed that must be positively unhealthy.

'If you mean is it flooding my cellar, yes, it is. Or it was this morning. I live in hopes that it might subside while I'm not there to glare at it.'

'On the other hand,' he suggested, and his voice was lower, more intimate as he bent his dark head closer to hers, 'it might take the opportunity, as soon as your back is turned, to burst its confines and carry your house off on the crest of a tidal wave—all the way from the sea, up the Thames, across London and down your street.'

She looked in the other direction and tapped her pen on the table in irritation. 'That seems highly unlikely. And I take my domestic matters seriously, Professor Mayer, even if you can afford not to have any.'

'Who says I don't have any?' Something at the edge of his tone caused her to glance quickly at him; but there was the glint in his eyes, the twitch at the corner of his mouth, which told her he was being flippant. 'I apologise for jesting at the expense of your property, Dr Hope. I can see that this business upsets you deeply.' She glanced at him again, but this time he appeared perfectly serious. 'I can only repeat my earlier request to be allowed to investigate the phenomenon for myself, in the interests of my researches. Perhaps I might even be able to bring the past to life for you—make you see that such an event has its positive aspects as well as its worrying ones.'

'Bricks and mortar are my only concern.' Tess wished

he would move farther away. 'But when it comes to bringing the past to life,' she went on firmly, determined to drag the conversation back to more impersonal realms, 'I can assure you my Mediaeval course is designed to do just that.'

'So I understand.' He grinned again. 'Is that your subtle way of reminding me why we're here? Would you rather discuss that?'

'Not particularly. Not until the others get here, at least.' She looked at the clock on the wall. 'They're always late,' she grumbled. 'Bill Jones makes a point of being half an hour after everyone else,' she said scornfully, 'but Prof Slocombe ought to know better.'

'It strikes me, Dr Hope, that you're not in the habit of showing a proper respect for your superiors.' The gleam in his eye was only just echoed in his tone. '*Professor* Slocombe is a much admired man in his field.'

'I'm not unaware of that. I've worked with him for several years, remember?'

He considered her thoughtfully. 'So—we men have to prove our worth directly to you, in person, is that it? No resting on our laurels, letting our reputation carry its own weight?'

Tess rummaged in her bag, found her reading-glasses and rammed them on her nose. Somehow they made her feel safer. 'What gives you that idea? I judge by what I find—first-hand experience. People's reputations don't cut much ice with me.'

'And has your first-hand experience taught you to be suspicious of *all* men, Dr Hope, whatever their reputation?' His voice had sunk so low it was almost a whisper. His face was disconcertingly close to hers; his arm resting against hers on the table-top. She wished to goodness the others would arrive and defuse this ridiculously charged atmosphere; how it had got like this she couldn't imagine. 'And you needn't think hiding behind those specs makes a jot of difference to the fact that you're a very attractive lady,' he announced unexpectedly. 'Quite a special one, in fact. Is there really any need for us to clash over a trivial professional point—Tess?'

She opened her mouth to reply, thought better of it, and closed it again. She could feel colour rushing to her cheeks—something which very rarely happened to her. Furious with herself as well as with him, she stood up and walked deliberately over to the window, conscious of his gaze following her every move. 'It's far from trivial, Professor Mayer—to me, if not to you. I realise you're only here for a short time, and that you're used to everyone running round in circles when you appear, reorganising their lives, rescheduling their timetables, bowing and scraping in honour of your . . . *reputation*!' She spat out the word as if it was an insult, turning to face him as she said it. 'But I don't subscribe to such sycophancy. I like to take people as I find them: men or women, it's all the same to me.'

That wasn't quite true, and she knew it; and so did he. But it suited her to make the blanket statement at this moment. His persuasive tactics were just another ploy in his campaign to take over her course, she knew that; and she wasn't having any of it. He wasn't getting round her that way.

'If you insist, *Dr* Hope,' he conceded gravely; and she was saved from further embarrassment by the arrival of Professor Slocombe.

'I'm so sorry I'm late, Professor Mayer,' he puffed as he sat himself heavily down at the table. 'Found myself delayed by a bunch of irritating . . . freshmen.' There was something ingratiating about the way he used the American expression for first-year students, Tess thought—as if he was determined to impress their transatlantic visitor. And don't bother to apologise to *me*, will you, her mind complained stridently; I'm only a mere lecturer, and a woman at that. But she simply smiled when he greeted her. 'Dr Hope, how are you today? Domestic—er—difficulties cleared up?'

'Not exactly, Professor. But I'm fine, thank you,' she returned politely.

'Good, good.' He beamed at both of them. 'Been getting to know each other a little—er—better? See any path out of the—er—jungle?' he enquired hopefully.

'Of course there is,' Joshua Mayer reassured him expansively. 'Dr Hope and I are beginning to see eye to eye already.'

Were they indeed? Refusing to meet his mocking glance, Tess looked away. But Professor Slocombe was delighted. 'That's the style! That's the ticket! No road so long it has no turning!' he declared platitudinously. 'No river so wide it can't be crossed!' Tess was quite used to his tendency to talk in proverbs when slightly pushed; but she could have wished he had chosen a different example. All this talk of rivers was getting her down.

At last her opposite number—the Mediaeval Lecturer in the History Department—arrived, and they could get on with the discussion. Bill Jones was thin, bearded and scruffy. Shy and highly intellectual, he was a great favourite with his students and a champion of all their most radical causes. He spent more time fighting and demonstrating in favour of one campaign or against another than he did actually teaching; but his work was of such a high standard that his political activities were cheerfully tolerated.

Tess liked Bill, and hoped she could get him on her side in this affair. He was well known as a supporter of equal rights for all, for one thing—if she could make him see the issue as a blow to her feminist pride . . . but then again, she warned herself, it wouldn't do to make too much of that argument, since she had already hotly denied to Joshua Mayer that it had anything to do with her gender. She frowned. Why did it have to get so complicated, when one was only trying to prove a simple point?

'Sorry, all.' Bill grinned at Tess, nodded to the two men. 'Got held up. What's it all about, anyway?'

'First, Dr Jones, have you met your new colleague, Professor Mayer, who has taken over from . . .'

'Oh yes, we've met,' Joshua Mayer cut in. 'At the cocktail party the Department so kindly laid on to welcome me.' Bill nodded his agreement.

'Well then, formalities can be dispensed with, since we are all—er—acquainted. Now, as I see it,' Professor Slocombe began briskly, 'the situation is this . . .' and he proceeded to describe Tess's course—its origins, its aims and achievements, its ingredients and methods—in such minute detail and at such length that she was sure all three of them would be fed up with the whole subject before they were much older.

'. . . and without causing severe disruption or in any way suggesting that Dr Hope should—er—move over in favour of anyone else, the Academic Board feels . . .'

'. . . that it should be a History, rather than an English, course?' Bill suggested in an attempt to get to the point.

'Oh, no, not that—not quite. Not entirely. You see . . .' Professor Slocombe was getting himself tied in knots. Tess made no move to disentangle him; he had got them into this mess, and he could get them out of it. Joshua Mayer sat, head to one side, listening carefully as if it was the most vital issue in the world to him. No wonder he was such a raging success, she mused; it was an art, making one tiny course in one insignificant department in one college seem so important, when it clearly wasn't worth a jot beside his hundreds of other interests and concerns.

'The point, as I understand it, Dr Jones,' he interrupted now, courteously, 'is this. We have no wish to change the basic meat of Dr Hope's excellent curriculum—which I have studied carefully,' he added, his expression impassive. 'Nor to give the impression that she is being ousted from her central position within it. But there is a feeling that the History Department might have some further light to shed on the topic of Mediaeval Studies—even more relevant information to impart than she already so ably does. Is that right, Professor?'

The Dean of Arts nodded gratefully. 'Exactly, Professor. The question is . . .'

'. . . how do we achieve such an analgamation, without detracting from the merits of the material as it stands; without causing grief to our colleague here, or her students; while at the same time being seen to be taking action according to the parameters specified by your Board, in their wisdom?'

Really, Tess thought grudgingly, he was a past-master at this sort of thing! Professor Slocombe was staring at him in open admiration. 'That's just it.'

'Well, I have a proposal which might suit all parties,' went on Joshua Mayer smoothly. He leaned back in his chair, long legs stretched out in front of him, hands nonchalantly in pockets. On the table before him lay a single sheet of notepaper with the four words: *General Arts—Medieval Studies* scribbled at the top. Tess stifled a pang of irritation at his Americanised spelling of her own subject. It was irrational, she knew; but it was almost as if he took a delight in underlining as many discrepancies as possible between their ways of looking at things.

Professor Slocombe radiated relieved approval. There was nothing he liked better than a lively newcomer who walked in and got things done. He himself seemed to have the greatest difficulty in getting anyone to do anything; he wasn't sure why. 'Tell us about it, Professor Mayer,' he urged.

Their visitor did not need to be pressed. 'I have gone into the timetable for this course very closely,' he expounded. 'And it appears to me that far too much material has been compressed into too few teaching hours. I realise it is a General Degree and not an Honours; but all the same, the students can hardly be expected to take in such a wide variety of information in—what is it?—two hours a week, including both lectures and tutorials?'

Tess agreed that it was. She could hardly deny that he had a point: it had never been easy to fit everything into the time allotted to her.

'Well then, the answer is simple. We—I—must persuade the powers that be to allow this course another hour a week at the very least. Their History curriculum is not, in my opinion, being employed to full capacity. It should be possible to move an hour over from—say—the Colonial Wars, or the Forging of the Empire—which have, I notice, been allocated more time than all the rest put together,' he commented sardonically. 'We could then ask Dr Hope to continue uninterrupted with her study of the period and its literature; but we could take some pressure off her by adding in something more on the general background of the era—the international scene, for example, which has been somewhat neglected up to now . . .' he looked around, aware that he had captured their attention.

'More on politics, less on the human angle,' Bill Jones suggested thoughtfully. 'Well, that's my field, certainly, but would you feel . . . taken over, Tess?' He looked at her doubtfully.

She smiled at him; he hadn't missed the complex undertones of the situation. Perhaps her postgraduate student, Mike, had been having words in his ear about her first reaction. 'Not by you, Bill,' she replied pointedly. 'It would hardly be your fault. This decision has nothing to do with you.'

'Perhaps I should remind you,' Joshua Mayer pointed out tersely, 'that it has nothing to do with me directly, either. We are all simply endeavouring to implement a directive from On High.'

'Absolutely,' endorsed Professor Slocombe. 'As Dr Hope well knows, it was not my idea in the first place. But may I say that I think Professor Mayer's suggestion is first-class.' He looked pleadingly at his two junior colleagues. 'Don't you?'

'I can't see anything against it—if Tess doesn't mind, and as long as the students are in favour,' said Bill in his mild voice. 'I always believe in full consultation with the student body.'

'We are aware of that, Dr Jones,' Professor Slocombe remarked, allowing a hint of his customary dryness to surface, now that things appeared to be working out satisfactorily. He turned to Tess. 'And you, Dr Hope?'

She had been unconsciously doodling on her notes with a pencil. Now she took her glasses off and chewed an earpiece as she often did when she was busy thinking. It had seemed a fair enough proposal—annoyingly fair, even. None of her time nor subject matter was taken from her; only a wider backdrop was to be added to it. What was more, she was in no doubt that Professor

Joshua Mayer would have no trouble in persuading the authorities to implement it.

But she was strangely loath to concede a point to him. It was too much like conceding defeat. She risked a quick glance in his direction: the grey eyes were firm and steady on her face—serious, searching, but somehow, she felt sure, taunting. 'I suppose it could be worked out,' she ventured.

'Of course it could.' For the first time, an element of impatience entered the suave American drawl. 'I myself will be on hand to ensure that it is implemented this semester. Dr Jones and I will, between us, draw up a suitable syllabus—with the co-operation of Dr Hope, of course. Then, when I leave, Dr Jones will be more than qualified to take over the whole shooting match. How does that sound?'

'Fine, fine.' Professor Slocombe could barely disguise his delight. It had all gone so much more smoothly than he had dared expect. These young female academics could be so . . . temperamental. He had been afraid he might be up against a battle royal with Tess Hope. Dealing with women had never been his strong suit; but it seemed their American colleague was more than ready for the challenge. 'I'm extremely grateful to you, Professor Mayer.'

'Not at all, Professor Slocombe.'

'I hate to interfere with this male mutual admiration society,' Tess observed, and her voice was taut, 'but I haven't actually agreed yet.'

Her professor's face fell. Perhaps his jubilation had been premature. 'But I thought . . .'

'I fail to see what else we can do for you, Dr Hope, short of wrapping you in cottonwool in order to protect your delicate feelings.' Joshua Mayer's veneer of patience had worn very thin; and now he let his irritation overflow. The effect was alarming; to Tess, however, it merely served as the proverbial red rag to the bull.

'My delicate *female* feelings, no doubt you mean,' she flashed back. 'I assure you again that my stance in this matter had nothing to do with those—nothing whatsoever. I simply felt slighted . . . passed over.' Sitting up very straight, she braced herself to glare boldly into those steel-grey eyes. 'But I am, since you ask me, able to see the logic of your proposal, Professor Mayer. I accept it with thanks and without reservation. Once I am settled down to work with Dr Jones—the sooner the better,' she added meaningfully, 'I'm sure we can make a success of it. And then the whole affair will be easily seen as what it really is—a storm in a teacup.' She tossed her head defiantly. Sometimes it was necessary to give way gracefully; sometimes you had to lose a battle in order to win the war. Instinct told her this was one of those times.

'Splendid!' Professor Slocombe's good humour was instantly restored. 'We'll take it from there, then, shall we?' He was anxious to call an end to the meeting before she changed her unpredictable feminine mind.

'I must say,' Joshua Mayer was staring at her speculatively, 'I admire your ability to see things rationally, Dr Hope.'

She turned her most charming smile full on to him. 'For a woman,' she agreed sweetly, 'I can be remarkably rational, as I'm sure my male colleagues would admit.'

'Oh, indeed.' Professor Slocombe fell unwittingly straight into her trap. 'Dr Hope is a most—er—reasonable young lady. I was saying so only last evening, was I not, Dr Hope?'

'You certainly were.' She transferred the sickly smile to him. 'And now, if you've all finished with me, can I go? I still have a pile of essays on *Piers Ploughman* to wade through before I can get back to my domestic pursuits. Those little feminine things we bother our fluffy head with.' She stood up and collected her papers together, carefully avoiding everyone's eyes.

Bill Jones got up too. 'I'll come with you, Tess. I'd like to talk to you a bit more about this, if you've got a moment.'

'We shall meet again in due course, then,' Professor Slocombe suggested anxiously, 'when Professor Mayer and Dr Jones have concocted a suitable syllabus?'

'Whenever you say.' Tess felt her new docile front lending her a sort of spurious power. She rather liked it; it was far less exhausting than the perpetual struggle. 'Excuse us, then, gentlemen.'

Both eminent professors rose to their feet as she left the room, and Bill loped after her. Without looking directly at him, she caught the expression on Joshua Mayer's face: the brows gathered over the hooked nose were deeply pensive, the eyes meditative. She could feel their intense beam like a physical touch on her back as she closed the door on them.

CHAPTER FOUR

WEEKENDS were always a welcome relief to Tess. She enjoyed her college work, but she put a lot into it. She valued the opportunity to relax and retrench; to catch up on some of her domestic chores; and just to enjoy her own company for a few hours. Then there were usually piles of essays to mark, and the next week's lectures to prepare. As far as she was concerned, those two days off seemed to fly by all too fast.

This Saturday morning she decided to tackle some of the grimier tasks about the house—the ones that always got put off until they had to be faced. If her cellar floor was still lurking beneath an inch of water, that was no reason why the rest of the place should be neglected. She rolled up her sleeves, put on her oldest jeans and a loose cotton overshirt, tied her black curls into a bright red bandanna, and got on with the job.

She had cleaned the cooker—the worst chore of all—and was perched on a high stool wiping down some top shelves in the kitchen, when the doorbell rang. Fritz, who was curled up on top of the central heating boiler, half opened one eye, stretched, draped an elegant paw across his nose and went back to sleep.

'Huh!' Tess muttered, jumping down from her stool and rinsing her dirty hands under the tap. 'It's okay for some. Why can't you do something useful for a change, like answer the door? All intake and no output, that's your trouble!'

She turned down the radio, which was regaling her with mindless pop music—the kind she hated except when it provided a bland background to her thoughts and activities. She didn't bother to wipe off the smudges that would inevitably have appeared on her face in the course of her scrubbings and polishings. It was probably only the milkman. Not that she had anything against milkmen—hers was a cheery soul, always ready with a quip and a bit of gossip, but not worth tidying up for. Or perhaps it might be Mrs Jacobs, next door but one, come to leave her keys so that Tess could feed her cat while she went off for the weekend.

She opened the door—and backed into the hall, quite unprepared for the sheer size of her visitor, let alone his identity. He loomed on the doorstep, filling the doorway: Joshua Mayer—his expression sardonic, his hair windblown and his broad frame casual in jeans and a thick black sweater. One hand grasped a dark leather briefcase; a set of car-keys jingled in the other. Behind him, parked against the kerb, Tess caught a glimpse of a streamlined saloon car—shining yellow, with darkened windows. That would give the neighbours something to talk about!

'Professor Mayer!' She gawped at him stupidly. 'I wasn't . . . I didn't . . .' She glanced down at her old clothes, her stained and grubby appearance.

'Naturally you were not expecting me, Dr Hope. If you had been, I don't suppose you would have answered the door at all—would you?' Gimlet-like, the grey gaze drilled itself into her face.

'Well—that is, I don't know,' she mumbled—trying desperately to recapture her usual articulacy in the face of this unwarranted intrusion.

'Go on, you know you wouldn't. I'm not exactly your favourite person right now—I know that,' he drawled. 'But now that I'm here, are you going to ask me in? Or are you going to slam the door in my face?'

With an effort she regained some of her poise, re-membering—just in time—her latest tactic: that air of aloof acceptance. 'I hope I've got better manners than that, Professor. Won't you come in?' she invited tautly.

She stepped back to allow him to enter: his presence dwarfed the compact hallway. His brows were gathered into their expression of quizzical surprise; his voice was low, offhand. 'I must say, I didn't expect to be greeted so . . . warmly,' he remarked.

'Hardly warmly. But with a modicum of politeness, I hope.'

'Oh yes,' he mocked, his eyes never leaving her face, 'you British are renowned world-wide for your . . . politeness—in the most unlikely contingencies.'

'And why not? What's wrong with that?' she de-manded heatedly; then she bit her lip, reminding herself of the cool front she was maintaining, and manufactured a stiff smile. 'Will you have some coffee? I was about to make myself some.'

'That would be delightful, Dr Hope. Thank you,' he accepted solemnly.

'I'm having a clean-up session, as you see,' she ex-plained unnecessarily, leading him into the cosy kitchen. 'As long as you don't mind sharing it with me in these domestic quarters. Not your normal . . . scene, I dare say.' She allowed herself the one quick barb.

'Didn't anyone ever tell you it was foolish to jump to conclusions on slight evidence?' he replied, his scrutiny leaving her now to inspect the room. 'As it happens, I'm most interested in kitchens; and in cooking too, humble male though I am. This is very pleasant,' he pronounced, with the air of an expert. 'I like it. It's very . . . you,' he added inscrutably.

The sincerity in his tone was unarguable, but Tess felt curiously deflated by his words. He was right, of

course—you should never judge people by their superficial appearances. 'Do sit down.' She indicated the
wooden chairs, drawn up at the table, and he sat on one
of them, none the less overpowering for being down at
her level. 'To what do I owe the honour?' She busied
herself with the kettle, her back towards him.

'I thought you might ask me that. Well . . .' he opened
his briefcase and took out a folder, 'as it happens, I was
in the vicinity, following up a line of research.'

'And what was that?' She spooned coffee grounds into
her earthenware pot.

'You won't be in the least surprised to hear that it's
your friend and mine—the River Fleet.'

She turned round to face him, eyebrows raised cynically. 'Quite a coincidence!'

'You have every right to be sceptical, Dr Hope. I
admit that it was your story which brought it to the front
of my mind; but it's an angle I've studied in other cities,
and I had every intention of looking into it here, in due
course. Your . . . experience simply encouraged me to
do it sooner rather than later.'

She poured boiling water on to the grounds. 'So
you're still after a look at my private tributary of the
Fleet—if that's what it really is,' she added, a thread of
anxiety running through her tone.

'Any further developments on that front?' He
accepted the mug of coffee she handed him.

'Not a thing. It sits there, or rather, it runs sluggishly
there; and I wait up here. The Water Board haven't been
in touch, and they promised they would as soon as they
found anything. I wasn't supposed to contact them again
unless it did anything dramatic, and it hasn't—so . . .'
She shrugged gloomily, sitting down opposite him,
keeping a cautious distance between them.

He refused milk and sugar before sipping his coffee.

'Mmm—good.' He smiled his appreciation. 'I have to say it—making coffee is not one of your great British skills. It's never strong enough for me—and nearly always that horrible instant stuff. This is more like it. I congratulate you, Dr Hope.'

'It's my one concession to luxury in these stringent times, Professor Mayer.'

'About this river of yours.' He sounded eager. 'May I see it?'

'Since you're here, I don't see why not.' Tess regarded him suspiciously. 'You say you were in the area anyway?'

'I decided to take myself to see the source of the Fleet, then follow its path as far as I could. When I studied the old maps . . .' he pointed to the bundle of documents he had taken from his case, ' . . . and realised just how near it took me to your home . . .'

'That's a point,' Tess interrupted, sitting bolt upright as a sudden thought struck her. She was crazy not to have worked it out earlier. 'How did you know where I live?'

His mouth twitched slightly. 'I'm not above making use of college records. Nothing confidential, of course— but it's not so difficult to persuade someone to reveal such information. In this case, it was the college librarian—I told her I needed to contact you urgently and you'd gone home.' He cast his eyes down in mock penitence. 'Dastardly, wasn't it?'

'Cheeky, certainly.' She hardly knew whether to be flattered or horrified. He must have been keen to locate her if he had gone to such lengths. 'Well, you might have let me know. I could have . . .'

'Baked a cake? Put on your glad-rags? Made sure the door was padlocked and the place booby-trapped?' He grinned sardonically. 'No way, Doc Hope. I wasn't

taking any chances. I wanted to catch you unawares—
and that's just what I did, I believe,' he added with
satisfaction, his glance openly dwelling on her working
clothes.

'You know perfectly well you did!' She glared at him.
'Okay, so you did a bit of sleuthing—nothing to be proud
of, I'd have thought. Anyway,' she observed caustically,
'I might have been out. Had you thought of that? I do
have shopping to do—I even have a social life of my
own,' she assured him.

'You might indeed. I was prepared to risk that disappointment—there's always another day.' The grey
eyes glinted lazily at her from over the rim of his coffee
cup. 'And now that I've taken such liberties already,' he
went on, 'don't you think it's about time we dropped all
this "doctor" and "professor" stuff? I mean, I know we
have a serious professional relationship, but isn't this
taking formality a bit far, even in England? Here I am, in
your home, accepting your hospitality . . .'

'. . . through no invitation of mine,' Tess reminded
him sharply.

'Correct. But even so . . .' His voice was warm,
persuasive. She could imagine him only too clearly,
getting round Jenny, the college librarian. 'Could you
not bring yourself to address me as Joshua—or even, if
you feel really daring, Josh?' He was teasing her now, his
tone stiffly formal. 'And might I, perhaps, be permitted
to call you Tess?'

She looked down at her hands clasping the chunky
coffee mug. This whole thing seemed to be leaping out of
her control. They had only met twice, after all—and in
less than favourable circumstances. She knew nothing
whatever about the man: his private life, his background
. . . but perhaps there was no harm in breaking down the
barriers that much, at least. What was in a name?

'After all,' he remarked airily, 'what's in a name?'

Tess glanced up at him. It was one thing for him to penetrate the inside of her house—something very few of her work colleagues ever did; but it was quite another when he started stepping into her head. She prided herself on the well-guarded privacy of her thoughts from the world.

'Okay—Joshua.' The name felt strange on her tongue. She managed a brief grin, which he returned.

'Great—Tess. That's better; a whole lot better. We need to be on amicable terms,' he reminded her, 'if we're to work side by side on this Mediaeval course.'

'I suppose so,' she agreed coldly.

'You don't sound too delighted about that, Tess. Didn't you think my solution was in everyone's best interests?'

'Oh, it was brilliant. A brilliant piece of . . . diplomatic manoeuvring.' Her brown eyes held his, sparking. 'Who could have failed to admire it?'

'You're still sore at me, aren't you, Tess?' He leaned across the table; and suddenly one of her hands had become imprisoned under one of his, lying on the scrubbed wooden top. She stiffened all over at the touch of it; a creeping paralysis threatened, starting at the toes and working its way up.

'Of course I'm not,' she managed to mutter. Her hand was rigid, stuck where it lay, inside his. She didn't even dare to wiggle her fingers in case that increased contact with his skin, only adding to the intensity of her reaction. This was ridiculous: it was only a hand, after all. He was only a man. She did not go in for . . . this sort of thing; he had got the wrong person if he thought . . .

He released the hand as abruptly as he had seized it, suddenly brisk. 'Before I forget,' he rummaged among his papers, 'I have another errand too—I want to show

you this. I found it in my files. I thought you might prefer
to keep your business and your domestic affairs strictly
separate, being the thoroughly professional lady you
are . . .' Was there still the hint of a taunt in the
smooth, deep voice? 'So I brought it here with me
instead.'

'Very considerate of you,' Tess said carefully. What
was he up to now? The man and his motives were as
mysterious to her as the water in her cellar—and both
had arrived in her life with equally disconcerting lack of
warning.

'Ah yes, here it is.' He produced a sheet of paper
on which a short poem had been photocopied. 'I remembered this from when I was doing some similar
research in the States. It's by my compatriot, Robert
Frost—perhaps you know it; you're the literary expert.
It seems to sum up exactly what I was trying to say to
you.'

She took the paper from his hand and tried to concentrate her attention on it. With his gaze sharp upon her it
wasn't easy, but she made a supreme effort. The poem
was called *A Brook in the City*. It had been printed above
a small line drawing of an old country house surrounded
by towering modern buildings.

> *The farm house lingers*, it began, *though averse to
>   square*
> *With the new city street it has to wear*
> *A number in.*

Tess read it to herself, then looked up at him. He was
watching her, a warmth now softening the shrewd eyes,
the sharpness of the eagle's beak, the powerful features.
'Go on,' he encouraged, 'read it aloud.'

Tess took a deep breath, and read:
> *'But what about the brook*
> *That held the house as in an elbow-crook?*
> *I ask as one who knew the brook, its strength*
> *And impulse . . .'*

She glanced up at him again, her face lit by a thrill of recognition. He was smiling now. 'I like to hear you read. You have a lovely accent.'

She had an accent? That was a new way of putting it; Tess had rather assumed him to be the one with the accent. Of course, just like most other things, it depended entirely where you were standing. It was always the other person, her mind pointed out, who was out of the ordinary—the exception; never oneself.

She pushed the poem towards him across the table. 'Your turn. You're a fellow-American—and a fellow-male. Let me hear how he wanted it to sound.'

He took it without demur, and read the rest in his rich, mellow tones. Tess listened, enthralled, to Frost's description of how the fields had been *cemented down from growing under pavements of a town* . . .

Glancing up at him covertly, she watched Josh's face as he read: the profound grey of the eyes, the knitted brows, as he identified with the words he was reading. It was hard, for a moment, to tell where the poet ended and the reader began. How, Frost demanded, in Josh's voice, should we *dispose of an immortal force no longer needed?* Why should this innocent stream have been . . . *thrown*

> *Deep in a sewer dungeon under stone*
> *In fetid darkness still to live and run—*
> *And all for nothing it had ever done*
> *Except forget to go in fear perhaps . . . ?*

He paused. 'In fetid darkness,' she repeated slowly. 'That's marvellous. It sheds a whole new light on the subject, Josh,' she admitted.

'Would you listen when I tried to say something to that effect myself?' he complained. 'But then I'm no poet. Now, this is where I come in—get this:

No one would know except for ancient maps
That such a brook ran water . . .'

Triumphantly, he broke off to wave a handful of papers at her. 'See? Here they are: the "ancient maps"—that's where we historians come in.'

'I never doubted it,' she assented coolly. His jubilation seemed out of all proportion; but he was clearly a volatile man.

'If I were a river,' he continued, thoughtful now, 'and someone did that to me—pushed me "*deep in a sewer dungeon under stone*"—I'd make good and sure I broke *my* way out.'

'Yes, I expect you would.' Tess surveyed him from under her lashes. 'No matter where—someone's cellar, or not—it would be all the same to you.'

'This bit, I'll have you know,' he informed her, 'was only imprisoned in its present pipes just over a hundred years ago. It can hardly have got used to being down there. You must treat it with a little sympathy.'

'Must I?' He was more than half in earnest, she could tell. It was strange—such a dynamic, realistic, modern man as he was, having this whimsical streak. She couldn't help softening towards him, seeing it. 'I've told you before—if it wasn't my property it had decided to surface in . . .'

'And now,' he demanded, standing up, businesslike, 'you can't refuse to show me the evidence—not after that. Let's see whether I can feel this stream's vibes, tell you if they're hostile or benign.'

'If you insist,' she sighed. 'There's not a lot to see, either way.' She led him to the cellar stairs. 'It's just . . . wet,' she concluded practically.

'I despair of you, Tess.' Josh's deep voice echoed as he followed her down the stone stairway. 'You have no soul!' He arrived beside her at the foot of the steps. 'I see what you mean, though. Definitely wet. Yes, wet: that's the word one would use down here.'

'I'm glad we agree on that, at least,' said Tess, a wry edge to her tone.

He bent down and peered at the water, testing it with one finger just as the Water Board man had done. Then he put his head on one side and murmured: 'Hmm.'

'Good grief!' she exploded. 'This is a conspiracy. That's exactly what the so-called expert said. Can't you find a more original comment to make?'

'I do apologise for my lack of originality, but there isn't a lot one can say about a river flowing through a cellar,' he pointed out acidly.

'Not when you're actually confronted with it, no. Now maybe you know how I've been feeling.' Tess looked up at him—eyes bright, black curls escaping from their scarf, cheeks pink in the dim light. 'But I'm surprised at you, Professor. I never imagined you at a loss for words—great man that you are, world-famous writer and speaker.' The smile in her voice was full of irony.

But he did not smile back; and for a moment she was afraid of the intensity, the fierce set of his mouth, the burning light in his eyes. She took a step away, involuntarily moving out of his reach, she was hardly sure why. But he caught hold of her, both strong hands on her shoulders, his eyes sharp on hers—suddenly, overpoweringly serious.

'Tess.' His voice was strange, guttural. She shivered in the dank subterranean atmosphere, now rooted to the spot under the pressure of his hands. 'Tess,' he whispered again, on an indrawn breath, 'are you going to keep . . . fighting me? Or are you going to accept the inevitable?'

'What do you mean?' she tried to say; but his face was leaning down, close to hers—closer. Her lips had become dry, stuck together; she moistened them in a nervous gesture with the tip of her tongue.

Josh's fingers dug painfully into her shoulders—those same long, delicate fingers she had noticed only a few days before. She struggled to keep cool against an onslaught of responses; but she was totally unprepared. Men had been this near her, often enough, but it had never really had much effect—she had felt detached, let them get on with it until she had had enough of their manhandling. Now, standing on a damp stone floor, in the middle of a Saturday morning, with oven grease on her nose and nothing but everyday matters in her head, her body was apparently about to let her down.

'Joshua . . . Josh,' she quavered, breathless. 'No—don't!'

'No? Don't?' his voice rasped out, in cruel imitation of her protests. His hands came up now to frame her face, forcing it to look up at his, those fingers firm around her cheeks and chin. 'You know as well as I do that this has been inevitable since the moment we set eyes on each other. Liberated lady as you are, Dr Hope, you can hardly deny that.' There was a harshness in his tone now, almost bitterness. 'Isn't that what liberated ladies like you are all about?'

Fear and anger fought against the deeper replies she could sense her body sending out to him, unbidden. 'You don't . . . understand . . .' It was hopeless: how to explain to him that he had got the wrong end of every stick—that, just because she was independent, lived alone, had modern ideas about the status of women, it didn't mean she was freely available? Or even sexually experienced?

Finally she mustered her spirit. 'You're all the same—*men*!' She spat out the last word as if it was the ultimate insult. 'You think you're God's gift to us all. That if you give us equal rights, out of the kindness of your hearts, that gives *you* the right to . . . reach out and grab what you want, when you want. Well, let me tell you here and now, *Professor*, that I'm not one of your feeble-minded pushovers. If that's what you were after when you came here, you're due for a big disappointment!'

The fingers were clamped tight on her jawbone, but she did not flinch. Her defiant gaze shot fire into his; but he gave as good as he got. 'For a mature, intelligent, educated woman,' he grated, 'you seem remarkably obtuse, Dr Hope—or else you must be remarkably dishonest. You can hardly expect me to believe you've been quite unaware of the messages I've been constantly receiving from you, each time we've been together?'

'If any part of me has been sending messages,' she retorted truthfully, 'my mind had nothing to do with it.'

'So . . .' His mouth was very close to hers, his breath warm against her face. Scents from him swamped her nostrils: a sharp tang of after-shave, soap, male skin. 'Mind over matter, is that it? Are you so securely tucked inside that pretty, overworked little head of yours that you aren't even tuned to what your body's telling you?'

'I can't . . . I won't . . .' Her hands pushed at his chest, but it remained hard, immovable—a wall of solid muscle.

'Then we'll have to change all that, won't we?' The full

power of his determination was compressed into the question, murmured against her lips. Before she could reply, his mouth was taking hers, profoundly, totally, in a way she had never imagined, let alone experienced.

Her hands gave up their unequal battle and clutched the front of his sweater for support. Her head was being bent back, back; and still Josh pressed, and ground, and claimed what he wanted to claim, until Tess was sure she would fall over backwards to the hard floor. But his hands left her face and grasped her round the waist, at once holding her up and pinning her down. She was successfully immobilised—a gasping fish on a hook, a butterfly pinioned to a board.

And then, without warning, it was over. Josh released her, flinging her back so that she landed against the cold wall of the cellar, one foot ignominiously in the water up to the ankle. For endless seconds she stared at him, conscious of her mouth exposed, trembling; knowing it would be swollen and bruised, and that there would be weals on her face and neck where his fingers had clenched her skin.

This was the moment to summon up all her rage and hostility. He had been brutal, unfeeling, fascist—taken advantage of her inferior physical strength; displayed every worst aspect of his sex, achieved dominance by force. But, for some reason, all her anger had deserted her—all the fury, the righteous indignation which she knew he deserved. All she felt was a numb disbelief. This sort of thing happened to other people not to Tess Hope.

Even worse, somewhere deep down inside her—she tried not to recognise or acknowledge it—there was a stirring, a flicker of something suspiciously like desire. That excitement, that glow which she had so seldom felt, lighting up some inner reach of her which had made its existence known to her only on rare occasions—and even then only the barest, most unfulfilled glimpse.

She lifted her head proudly. He must never know that; never. 'End of tutorial, Professor?' She forced her mouth to form the glib words. Her voice was husky, but at least it was there. 'Had enough? Have I . . . passed with a good grade?'

There was something like astonishment in his own stare; those dark, heavy brows meeting over the hooked nose, that wry twist to the long mouth. His hands raised themselves a few inches, in a gesture that was almost beseeching, and then dropped again to his sides. He opened his mouth and then closed it again. Her confidence gathered: it seemed he had even alarmed himself.

'Tess.' How different, how alien her own name sounded on that deep, urgent note! It seemed to have nothing to do with her at all. 'What can I say to you?' Josh cleared his throat; his voice was even more hoarse than hers. 'I don't usually—it's not my style to behave in that . . . uncivilised fashion. I don't usually need to . . .'

'. . . take women by force?' Tess jeered. 'I'm sure you don't.' Sarcasm permeated her tone now; she sensed she had the upper hand, despite his show of violence. Violence never paid off—wasn't that what she had always been taught? 'I'm sure you don't often have any trouble at all persuading members of my poor weak sex to . . . *come across*, isn't that the expression?' She smiled bitterly—and stiffly, feeling the stretch on her painful lips. 'Then it's about time you *came across* one, Professor Mayer, who isn't an instant victim to your charms. I'm glad to have been of some educational service to you, after all.'

'Tess, don't sound—like that.' The grey eyes implored; she could almost believe he was genuinely stricken with remorse. Almost, but not quite. 'I never meant it to happen that way . . . it's just that I . . . misconstrued you. Misread your . . . messages,' he explained drily.

'You've obviously got a thing or two to learn about women, even if I don't know much about men!' Her tone was sharp now; she realised, with relief, that the anger was building itself up at last. Now she knew where she was; she felt safe. 'This may be a liberated age, but being liberated means we can be free to pick and choose— whom we want, when we want. True liberation doesn't mean we have to be at the disposal of any man who happens to feel . . . to be . . .' she groped for the words.

'Randy? Horny?' he supplied, his own temper rising to match hers.

Tess flinched from the rawness of them. 'If you insist.'

'Don't like those, huh?' he taunted. 'Prefer euphemisms—like "turned on", or "aroused"? Or the sort of phrases you might read in lightweight fiction?' He grinned fiercely, his eyes scathing. 'I didn't put you down as a romantic, Tess Hope—maybe I should think again. Like I said earlier, appearances sure can be deceptive.'

A romantic? That was the last thing she was, surely? 'Don't be such a fool!' She stepped gingerly from the water, suddenly exhausted, and set off up the stairs. 'Of course I'm not a romantic. I'm a—a realist. But I do have to . . . feel something before I can—commit myself that way.' She was glad he could not see her face.

He was following close behind her, though; and his voice was soft, intimate in her ear. 'And how often have you . . . "felt something", Tess?' There was a pause; she did not deign to enlighten him—why should she? It was none of his business. 'How often?' They reached the top of the stairs and emerged into the warmth and light of the house. 'Not often—am I right? Not very often at all,' he mocked.

She glared at him, reddening. 'Not many men are worth it,' she told him flatly. 'And now, if you'll excuse me, I must change these shoes and socks. Then I'm going to make some more coffee,' she declared, 'and pretend this unfortunate scene never happened.'

'You're not just a romantic; you're an ostrich too.' He chuckled. Obviously, she reflected, his moods were fickle: contrition . . . anger . . . they swept through him like so many gusts of wind. 'You'll be telling me next you're not waiting for Mr Right to come along, sweep you off your feet, show you all those secrets your body has hoarded up for so many years, specially for him.'

'Not in the least.' Tess tried not to sound as uncomfortable as she felt. His cruel accusation did, after all, have a grain of truth lodged in it somewhere. 'I'm just—integrated, that's all. I've made a conscious decision to keep my heart and head, my mind and body, in tune with each other. Doing things for . . . kicks isn't where I'm at.' She used the slang phrases with prim, deliberate satire.

'You've got it all worked out, haven't you—in your head.' Josh regarded her pensively now; she was sure he could dissect all her thoughts. 'Where *are* you at, Tess?' He grabbed her arm, forcing her to look at him. 'Are you so sure you know?'

'Are *you*?' Using an old trick, she answered the impossible question with another.

He shrugged. 'Maybe not. It's kind of refreshing, I guess, meeting a lady like you, in this day and age. If you're really all you say you are. Or rather,' he added caustically, '*don't* say you are.'

'It's nothing to do with you, what I am,' she repeated. 'From now on, I suggest we both stick to our own lives, and keep our relationship on a strictly professional basis. Even that,' she observed, 'may not be the easiest part of the next few weeks. It was kind of you to call, Josh,' she went on, with forced brightness, 'and give me the benefit of your . . . expertise; but now you'll have to go. I have things to get on with.' She turned to go upstairs, her wet foot squelching unpleasantly.

'Not even another cup of coffee?' He pouted, like a spoilt, incorrigible child. Men were such children, the lot of them, she thought scornfully.

'I can hardly throw you out bodily,' she reminded him, 'since you've just proved so conclusively how much stronger you are than me—in that way, at least.' Her tone suggested there were other, far more important, ways in which to be strong; and he didn't display many of them.

Marching to the kitchen, she filled the kettle and put it on the gas, glad of the routine action, the familiar occupation to soothe her shaking hands. Shock was setting in; she needed that cup of coffee urgently.

Fritz, blissfully unaware of the scene he had missed, jumped down from his nest on the boiler and joined them. He padded over to Joshua and sniffed nosily around his ankles.

'Hi there!' He bent to stroke the cat. 'I was under the impression you lived alone,' he accused. 'Who's this? A surrogate child?'

Tess greeted this conjecture with the cool disdain it merited. 'Children are the last thing my life needs, thank you. No, this is my companion, Fritz.' She spooned out the coffee grounds. 'A lot less trouble than living with another human being, I assure you—of either sex.'

'Fritz?' The dark eyebrows lifted into the tangle of black hair. 'Fritz the Cat?'

'That's right.' She poured water on to the coffee.

'You know who he was, don't you?'

'I know there's a cartoon character of that name, yes.'

'Not just any old character. He's the only cartoon that ever earned an X-rating. Pornographic animation—great stuff, I've seen it—it was a cultural breakthrough in its day, as I recall.' His eyes were gleaming with amusement.

'I did know that, actually. I don't expect you to believe it, but I named Fritz long before that film came out. He was called after a great-uncle of mine. He had nothing to do with any other cat, pornographic or otherwise.'

'I'll believe you,' said Josh, 'thousands wouldn't. Hey, Fritz.' He picked up the warm orange bundle and set it on his lap. Fritz purred enthusiastically—treacherously, Tess thought grimly—kneading the denim jeans with his claws.

'Well,' Josh remarked, 'at least someone round here appreciates my attentions. You're a fine fellow, aren't you?' Tess averted her gaze from the way the long fingers travelled lightly over the sleek soft fur, ruffling the thicker parts under the chin and on the chest. 'So, you were named after an Uncle Fritz?'

Fritz purred affirmatively. Tess said: 'Yes, he was my mother's uncle.'

'Did you know him yourself?' He sounded genuinely interested.

'No.' She paused, stirring the coffee. 'Not even my mother knew him. He was . . . left in Germany before the war. His brother—my grandfather—made his get-away and came here. My mother was—is—half German. Her father married an English girl, and they lived up north. My mother came down to London when she married my father.'

'So Fritz died in the war?' He was still stroking the cat.

'Yes. In a concentration camp, along with all the rest of his family.'

There was a silence. Then Josh said: 'So did several

members of mine. We could be related, somewhere far back. My family came from Germany as well.'

They looked at each other. 'Well, at least we have one thing in common,' she commented lightly.

'A very important thing,' he agreed. 'We share a small stake in an ancient race. My parents fled to America,' he explained, serious now. 'I'm only a first-generation citizen—not like you.'

So that accounted for the slight undertones in his accent. American, laced with German, inherited from his parents. 'Are they still living?' she enquired politely.

'They sure are. Lively and active in their old age—a lesson to us all.'

'Did you lose . . . many relatives?' She set his coffee down in front of him.

'A good many.' His face was impassive. 'I never knew them, of course, but it stays with you, I think—somewhere in your racial consciousness. Makes you all the more aware of the inequalities there are in the world. Prejudice, victimisation. Not just against women, either.' He glanced at her. 'Other races get the worst deal, in my opinion.'

'I think everyone shares that feeling of . . . betrayal about it,' Tess said.

'Not quite everyone.' He drank his coffee. 'Another excellent cup. You must allow me to return the hospitality some time.'

'Where do you live, Josh—in London, I mean?' She was being careful to keep her tone casually conversational. Already the exchange in the cellar might never have been.

'I have a flat—in Hampstead, actually. Not so far away, you see—and well placed to investigate the pattern of North London's historical development. And of its waterways. Talking of which, would you consider coming with me to look at some places? Perhaps a bit of fresh air might do us both good.'

'I don't know.' She looked down at her feet. One of them was still acting as a soggy reminder of the events of half an hour ago. 'I don't think it . . .'

'Come on, Tess.' Josh was enthusiastic, persuasive. 'I'd like to take you out to lunch—maybe make it up to you a little, show you I don't have to be such an uncouth boor. That wasn't really me you saw down there.' He grinned, taking her off guard. 'Blame it on the river if you like—those vibrations, that pent-up energy.'

'I shall do nothing of the sort. You can take full responsibility for your own actions.'

'And you too—for yours?' he asked quietly.

'I always do,' she assured him. There was something tempting about his offer. Her equilibrium had restored itself remarkably quickly after the . . . incident. And she hardly ever got taken out to lunch.

'Where would we go?' she asked. 'What is it you want to see?'

'What I want us to look at is not far from here.' His tone was enigmatic. 'As for lunch—well . . .' he shrugged expressively, 'there's no shortage of good eating places in Hampstead. That's one thing you can say about it. I usually stay there because it's convenient.'

And expensive, she thought; but she managed not to say so. Pushing aside the faint warning signals that were trying to make themselves heard in her brain—without much success, for once—she made up her mind. 'Okay,' she agreed, 'I'll come with you. Give me half an hour to wash and change, get myself together, make myself respectable.'

'That's my girl!' Pleasure and surprise mingled in Josh's face. 'You could hardly help being respectable, Tess.' Was that an insult or a compliment? she wondered. 'But you look fine as you are,' he added gallantly.

'Don't be stupid—of course I don't.' She was a mess, and she knew it. 'Make yourself at home,' she invited. Her dry tone suggested it was a bit late for such niceties—but one had to keep up the conventions, hadn't one? Just at this moment, she wasn't quite sure of anything she had been sure of two hours earlier. 'I won't be long.'

'That's fine,' he told her. 'Fritz and I have plenty to talk about. Don't we, Fritz? He's going to tell me all about what it's like, living with you.'

The cat got up, turned a complete circle on Josh's lap, and sat down again in exactly the same spot, throbbing his agreement.

CHAPTER FIVE

FORTY minutes later, Tess was staring out at the bustling Saturday-morning shoppers from a new vantage point: the well-sprung, smartly-upholstered passenger seat of a shining yellow Renault. Its ride was fast and smooth—two features it shared with its present driver, she reflected wryly—as fast, at any rate, as the packed streets would allow.

She had splashed her burning face with cold water, showered and changed into a pair of fashionably loose canvas trousers, a thick-knit brown and orange pullover and her short, comfortable boots. Wherever it was Joshua Mayer wanted to go, she had the distinct impression it wouldn't be anywhere sophisticated or urbane—not if it had any connection with his friend the River Fleet. And if the restaurant he favoured turned out to be somewhere smart and fancy—well, it was too bad: they would have to accept her as she was.

She did give her glossy curls a good brush, though, and even went to the unusual extreme of putting on a little make-up—subtly applied, of course, so as not to be too obvious—she didn't approve of it, really—but just enough to disguise her pale cheeks and bruised lips, and boost her confidence. Then she grabbed her long woollen scarf and matching bobble-hat, and presented herself to her guest in the kitchen.

'Ready when you are, Professor.'

He had summed her up in silence, the grey eyes sharp on every detail; then he had unfolded his considerable length from its chair, after carefully decanting a complaining Fritz on to the floor. 'It will be a privilege to escort you, Doctor,' he had replied gravely.

It made a change, watching London go by from a car. Tess didn't often ride in one—and when she did, it was never as luxurious as this. 'Have you bought this fine beast, or do you hire it for the duration?' she asked him now.

'I've bought it. I'll be here several months, and in my experience it's always better to own your own transport. I usually buy a new one, fresh from the production line, still under guarantee; then I sell it when I leave.' His glance flicked from the road to her face. 'Do you drive?'

'No, I've never learned. I've never really felt the need, living here.'

'It adds a certain freedom to life, I find. Independence—something you might value, I suspect?' he conjectured blandly.

'It's possible to be reasonably mobile without having recourse to four wheels and a load of expensive, lead-belching petrol,' she retorted at once. 'I cycle.'

'Ah, a conservationist, to boot?' He grinned. 'You're a lady of strong principles, aren't you, Tess Hope? Moral fibre and natural fibre—have I got it right?' He grinned again, more widely. In profile, it gave him an almost saturnine appearance.

Tess turned her head away to gaze through her own window. 'I try to be.' Compressing her lips into a tight (and still quite painful) line, she made a purposeful effort not to let herself give way to his needling. She had come through one challenge, not so many minutes ago; she would keep her dignity intact now, if it killed her. 'Where are we going?' she enquired mildly.

'Wait and see. Are you hungry, or shall we go there first?'

Tess considered. 'My appetite doesn't seem very

stimulated at the moment,' she confessed. 'Perhaps I need a bit of fresh air, as you suggested.'

'Perhaps you do. In which case, we shall very soon find some,' he promised.

He drove them through the more up-market reaches of Hampstead, where the houses were more like country mansions and the roads quiet and select. Tess had always regarded this area of London with a mixture of envy and resentment. Only the very wealthy could afford to own these residences, she knew. It didn't seem fair . . . but if anyone had offered her one, she would hardly have refused. 'Nice round here,' observed Josh, as if sensing the direction of her thoughts yet again.

'Nice, yes. Posh, but nice.' They turned neatly into a side road; he handled the vehicle and the route with practised, polished ease. 'You seem to know your way around pretty well, for a foreigner?' she suggested.

'Foreigner?' He frowned slightly. 'Hadn't thought of myself as that, exactly. Foreigner. Alien. Yes, I suppose I am.' There was a deeply serious note at the edge of the words. 'Maybe that's what I am everywhere I go—never long enough in one place to qualify as a citizen, or put down roots.'

'But surely you have roots in the States? Where you live?' Tess turned to stare directly at him in her surprise.

He shrugged. 'I guess I do. I know other cities almost as well as my own. London, for instance. I've been here so many times, I've lost count. I know it as well as I know New York. I don't belong in it, but I know it.' There was resignation in the deep voice now, tinged with bitterness.

Suddenly, for the first time, Tess was aware of an overwhelming urge to find out more about this man's real self, his personal life. She didn't even know, she realised with an unaccountable shock, whether he was married! But somehow it wasn't going to be easy, asking him outright—he wasn't the sort of man you could openly cross-examine; and she was grimly determined to hold on to her air of detached disinterest.

She made a cautious start. 'Don't you have any family? Apart from your parents?'

Josh drew up by the side of the road at the very edge of Hampstead Heath—a peaceful corner of that great oasis in the middle of inner London's northern suburbs, where fields and copses and grassy banks allow you to pretend for a little while that you are in the country. Switching off the engine, he turned to look her full in the eyes. 'I have two sisters, Ruth and Naomi—both younger, both married. I'm the proud and devoted uncle of two nieces and three nephews, to date. Is that what you wanted to know?'

Her eyes held his gaze firmly. 'What else should I want to know? Where do they all live? New York?'

'In or near. One lot live in Princeton, so I see plenty of them. Not only my brother-in-law, but my sister as well, are teachers at the University. The place is crawling with us!'

'Must be a formidable force,' commented Tess sweetly.

He ignored the interruption. 'The other sister isn't far away—upstate, more rural. She married a rising young lawyer who's now risen and older. We all see a lot of each other, when I'm around. Which is hardly half the year,' he added, a trifle wistfully.

'That's great,' she said, with some feeling. 'I always wanted sisters and brothers. I hated being an only child.'

His eyes narrowed thoughtfully. 'An only, were you? No sibling rivalry? No healthy competition—no sharing?'

She shook her head. 'That's right. It explains my innate selfishness.'

He smiled; and it was unexpectedly warm. 'Not selfish, Tess. Self-aware, maybe . . . even selfconsciously individualistic. Nothing wrong with that.'

She experienced a physical tremor at the accuracy of his understanding of her character. No one had the right to have such insight after—what was it—three meetings. Three meetings! Was it possible? 'Are you some kind of psychologist in your spare time?' she hedged, retreating from the directness of his gaze and his words.

'Strictly on an amateur basis. When someone interests me enough.'

Tess stared out of the window at the inviting stretches of green, with splashes of gold where the trees were succumbing to autumn. A pale sun was attempting to light up a paler sky; weak rays filtered through the metropolitan haze, fingering patches of lush long grass and rich brown earth. It had been a wet season. 'Let's go, shall we?' she suggested. Further investigations of his private life would have to be postponed: she wasn't one to delve without encouragement.

He got out of the car and strode round to open her door. 'Thanks,' she muttered, climbing out.

Josh bowed mockingly. 'Think nothing of it. I like to tell myself there's still a place for chivalry—even in the life of the modern woman.'

'You could have fooled me!' she flung back, before she could prevent herself.

His expression darkened. 'I thought we'd agreed on a truce about that. I've told you, Tess, even I am subject to misapprehensions. Crossed wires; jumbled codes. Accept my apology and forget it, can't you?'

She looked away at the rolling landscape. 'I'll accept your apology, Josh.' Forget it, she suspected, she wouldn't. 'Now, where do we go from here?' she asked briskly.

'You mean literally or metaphorically?' he teased.

'Literally.' She blushed, furious with herself even as she did it. 'This is the Vale of Health, right?'

'Right,' he affirmed.

'Well, have we come here for the good of our souls, or our physical wellbeing?'

He set off downhill at an energetic pace. 'Both, I hope. One of the main tributaries of the Fleet rises right here, near the Vale. I always like to explore every aspect of the subject I'm dealing with for myself. Even if there's not much to see, I like to go to the spot, pick up the atmosphere, familiarise myself with the . . .'

'. . . vibes?' Tess skipped to keep up with his stride.

'Precisely. If we walk this way, we should be following its course. The first we'll properly see of it will be at the bottom, at Hampstead Ponds.'

'I've seen those hundreds of times,' she pointed out.

'I never said I was going to show you anything new,' Josh reminded her. 'But it might make you look at an old friend a new way—and that's even better, wouldn't you say?'

She hadn't thought of it quite like that. 'I suppose so,' she agreed, a little doubtfully.

'Now, every time you come and look at these ponds,' he told her, 'you can tell yourself that the water they contain is, and always has been, part of the River Fleet. After leaving them, it flows down to where your friend Hilary lives, in Gospel Oak. If you put a message in a bottle, it would carry it underground, maybe right under her house.'

That did, certainly, place the whole thing on a more realistic level. 'But what about *my* bit of the Fleet?' She skipped again to catch up with him.

He slowed down and caught hold of her hand. The effect was electric: for a split second she stopped dead; then she walked on beside him, staring ahead. 'Sorry. I forget to match my pace—I'm not much good at sharing walks with people. Just shout at me if I go too fast.' At that moment she could barely have managed a whisper, let alone a shout; but he didn't appear to notice. 'Your bit of the Fleet,' he continued, 'is the other tributary. It rises in the grounds of Kenwood—I expect you know that pretty well too?' She nodded. 'Then it flows through the other ponds . . .'

'Highgate Ponds?' She found enough voice to show an intelligent interest in his profound knowledge of her home patch.

'The very ones.'

'I used to sail my boat on one of those when I was little. Is it really part of the Fleet?' Her poise had returned now; but the sensation of his hand enclosing hers was becoming more pleasant every minute. 'I had no idea.'

'There you are. That's what we social historians are for—to give people a new slant on their familiar haunts. I have my uses in life, after all.'

'I never suggested you hadn't.'

'Not in so many words, maybe.' Josh grinned sideways at her. 'Anyway, to return to the Fleet. Those ponds, according to my information, are actually old reservoirs. They go down in steps, as you've probably noticed— the river flows right through. After that it goes under Highgate Road, through Kentish Town and into Central London.'

'Whenever I catch a bus to work,' Tess realised, half to herself, 'I'm going along above some of it. And I never knew.' In spite of herself she was gripped by the idea. 'But you still haven't told me where *my* river comes in?'

'The Fleet has several smaller streams running into it from the north. Your private brook, in my opinion, is likely to be one of those.'

'Not the Fleet proper?' She couldn't help registering disappointment.

He swung her hand, grinning down at her, showing white teeth. 'Do I detect a stirring of excitement—even involvement—in this matter, at last? You astound me, Dr Hope. I never thought I'd win you round, proud pragmatist as you are.'

She pulled a face at him. 'Of course I'm involved. It's my house, isn't it? I have a right to know exactly what goes on underneath it.'

'A perfect right,' he acknowledged. 'And that's why I've brought you here.'

'I'd like to see it all on the maps,' she admitted. 'In black and white.'

'It will be my pleasure and privilege to show you. And to give you so much lowdown on this thing that you'll be the best educated person on the subject in north London. Quite possibly in the world. Except, of course,' he added solemnly, 'for myself.'

'Now that's a tutorial I might even look forward to,' she heard herself replying—and wondered whether she had heard herself right.

Not far from the bottom of the hill they found the stream—a slow, muddy trickle, but definitely a stream. Josh spread out his arms. 'There you are—the infant Fleet!' He sounded so proud, Tess thought, he might have been responsible for its existence himself.

They followed it to the ponds and stood at the edge of the largest one, staring down into its somewhat murky depths. It was hard to imagine this stretch of water as an early stage of a great river which had once flowed, open and untrammelled, across the width of London—almost as wide and free as the Thames itself. Tess felt a twinge of distress as the full realisation hit her: all that power and energy, that natural exuberance, hidden away, dark and deep, inside a metal pipe. No wonder it complained and grumbled, seeping its way into basements, pushing up road surfaces, even flooding foundations. She remembered Josh's words, that very morning: *'I'd make good and sure I broke my way out . . .'* Yes, she had to agree with him.

'Seen enough?' His voice, so close to her that she could feel it rumbling through her body, sliced into her reverie. 'Getting hungry yet?'

She looked up at him. The cool air had brought colour back to her cheeks; a sparkle had replaced the haunted, angry flash in her brown eyes. Her hair, under its hat, was a tumble of black curls. Apart from the slight swelling on her curved lips, you would never have guessed at the trauma she had so recently suffered.

She thought about his question. 'Yes. Yes, I am. What's the time?'

He pulled back his sleeve to consult a large, expensive watch, dropping her hand to do so. It felt cold, empty, away from his. How quickly one could get used to such small intimacies . . . how reassuring it was, how easy to forget all about being separate, independent, after all . . . 'One-thirty,' he said.

'Is it really? I only had a piece of toast, and that was . . .' she worked it out, '. . . nearly five hours ago. I suppose I must be hungry.'

Josh seized her hand again. It was a gesture so blatantly proprietorial, she knew she ought to resent it. But she didn't; she liked it. What was happening to her, for God's sake? 'Come on, then,' he ordered. 'Back to the car. We could walk to a restaurant from here, but then we'd be miles from the car afterwards.' He glanced closely at her face. 'Are you okay to walk up the hill?'

'Of course I am,' she declared. But halfway up, the hunger pangs suddenly made themselves felt; and by the time they got into the car Tess was exhausted and slightly dizzy.

There was concern in his expression as he settled her in and started up the engine. 'I had a feeling you were emptier than you thought. Women are all the same—never in touch with their gastrostats!' She was too limp even to argue with this blatantly untrue generalisation, merely leaning against her window, feeling its cool smoothness against her warm cheek. 'I know just the place for instant refuelling,' he went on, accelerating away from the Heath and back towards Hampstead Village. 'Do you like Italian food?'

'I like any food,' she assured him faintly.

'Good.' There was a short pause. 'I like a girl who likes her food. I've always reckoned it was a good sign.'

Tess was far too weary to enquire what it was a good sign of—which was probably just as well.

Within twenty minutes she was making inroads into an enormous, delicious pizza, piled high with tomatoes, olives and mozzarella cheese, crispy at the edges and doughy in the middle, just how a pizza should be. Four small bowls of different salads stood between them on the table. This was her idea of a perfect restaurant: you could help yourself to the salad selection, take as much as you liked and go back for more—if you had room. They were all fresh and imaginative; and if there was one thing Tess enjoyed, it was a good salad.

But today the hot solidity of the pizza was what she had needed. Now, her initial emptiness satisfied, she laid down her knife and fork and sat back to smile at her

companion—who was making a similar attack on a large
portion of lasagne. He paused, his fork halfway to his
mouth. 'Not full up already?'

'No, just resting. It's lovely, Josh—thanks.'

He refilled her glass with the highly palatable Rosso
they were sharing. She wondered whether she should
stop him: she very rarely drank in the daytime, and it
tended to make her chatter and then fall asleep. But she
felt so lightheaded already, there seemed little point in
making an issue of it. 'I like this place,' he was saying.
'It's less pretentious than some of these Hampstead
joints. I quite often come here.'

Tess started on the second half of her pizza. 'Is your
flat near here, then?'

He didn't answer at once, and she glanced up at him,
wondering if she had been too inquisitive. She caught a
fleeting expression of guarded anxiety before he allowed
his wide grin to break through again. Anxiety—and
what else was there? Pain, perhaps? Anger, even? The
man was certainly an enigma: was she about to find out
more? She forced herself into caution, although she was
burning with curiosity. 'Not far,' he said tersely.

That was about as uninformative as you could get. She
tried again—well fortified with dutch courage. 'Do you
always have the same flat, when you come to London?'
she asked.

'No. It belongs to a friend who's away in Japan for
fifteen months. He kindly said I could make use of it.' He
concentrated on his lasagne.

His evasiveness only intrigued her more. 'Is it . . .
big?' she tried archly.

The grey eyes levelled themselves on to hers. She took
a sip of wine to cover her confusion. 'Big enough for my
purposes,' he replied—an answer that was no answer.

She made one last-ditch attempt. 'Do you look after it

yourself? I mean, with everything you have to do, isn't it rather a lot of . . .'

'I manage perfectly well.' Poker-faced, he stared back at her. 'I've told you already, I'm more domesticated than you might think, for a humble example of that despicable sex I represent. I'm not a bad cook; and it's a service flat, so I don't need to worry too much about the more mundane aspects of everyday life.'

'Women's work, you mean?' Tess couldn't resist the dig. 'Like cleaning and washing? Lucky you.' She took another gulp of wine. 'Or perhaps,' she suggested boldly, 'you don't have to do all that in any case?' There could hardly be a more honest, ill-disguised probe than that. She had really put her cards on the table now; she hoped Josh would do the same.

Solemnly he told her: 'I've even been known to do some of that in my time. Contrary to your obvious suspicions, Tess, I'm no arch-male chauvinist.'

'I didn't think you were,' she replied untruthfully.

'I believe you did—and do.' She was sure his eyes were searching her soul; with an effort, she managed not to look away. Then, quite suddenly, he grinned. 'If this is a full-frontal attempt to find out whether I'm married . . .'

'Nothing was further from my mind!' she interrupted, even more untruthfully.

'. . . I'm here to inform you that I'm not, and never have been. And as far as I can see, never will be. Potential wives are not struck by the sort of peripatetic existence I lead. They like to have a base—roots. As we said before, I've never gone in for a settled life.'

There seemed to be no answer to this; so she helped herself carefully to some green salad. She wasn't sure what she had been expecting, if anything; but the news had sent a very peculiar thrill of pleasure through her, for some reason she preferred not to think too hard about.

'Are you surprised?' Josh asked, taking her off guard.

'That you're not married?' She shrugged, as nonchalantly as possible. 'I don't know—I hadn't given it much thought. I can see it would be a lot to expect a woman to take on . . . all that travelling . . . but if someone wants you enough . . .' She stopped, embarrassing herself by her own words.

'This sounds like a suspiciously romantic point of view,' he mocked. 'But I won't press the point,' he went on quickly, seeing her outraged expression. 'And I didn't say there hadn't been plenty of female company over the long years,' he pointed out before she could reply. 'There's usually some lady only too willing to oblige, in these free and easy times.' His tone was dry, almost sarcastic. 'I like women—I always have. There have been one or two I might have married; but they always wanted to settle down, and I wasn't the settling sort. I valued my freedom, more than I needed them, so . . .'

Tess speared a piece of cucumber as if it was her worst enemy; or perhaps as if it was the male sex. 'So you took what you wanted and left them to stew?'

'Hardly.' The dark brows lifted, the long mouth quirked. 'They did just as much . . . taking as I did, Tess. It takes two to tango, you know—to give, and to take. Or perhaps,' he said, putting his head on one side, 'you don't.'

'Don't what?' She toyed with a lettuce leaf, refusing to meet his eyes.

'Don't know. Haven't discovered yet that women can do their share of taking. Men aren't all hit-and-run operators.' He leaned forward, closer, conspiratorial. 'Don't breathe a word, but we have *feelings*, too!'

She hadn't ever given much thought to men's feelings. 'I suppose so,' she admitted, with a bad grace.

'You can bet your sweet life.' He smiled now, watching her expression. 'Hey, you look like you've had bad news. Did you want me to be a staid old married guy? Would it have made you feel safer, is that it?' Tess shook her head. 'Maybe you don't like my sordid history of torrid affairs?' he suggested softly. She pushed a piece of green pepper to the side of her plate with her fork, and said nothing. 'I'm thirty-seven years old,' he reminded her gently. 'I'm not made of stone. I have all kinds of . . . needs, as you so nearly found out for yourself.' She reddened; picking up her wineglass, for something to do, she drank some more. '*You* may be able to keep your heart and body . . . integrated, wasn't that the word? Some of us aren't quite so organised. Our baser instincts occasionally get the better of our fine intentions.' There was seriousness mingled with satire in his low tone.

'Men, especially.' She threw the accusation at him as if it was personal.

'Don't you believe it. Call yourself a liberated female? There are those, I can tell you, in all countries of the world, whose idea of freedom is less complex than yours. Who have learned to take what they could get out of life while they could get it. Whose needs—and appetites— are as strong as any man's.'

'I'll take your word for it,' Tess said coldly.

He drained his glass. 'Sorry—I've said too much. I've hurt you enough for one day. I was forgetting that under that cool exterior you're a simple, unspoilt girl. You don't want to be upset by talk of such raw aspects of life.'

She glared at him, infuriated. 'I can take it, Josh. Just because I don't . . . I didn't . . . that doesn't mean I don't know it goes on. I haven't been entirely protected from reality. Despite your earlier impression, I do not need to be wrapped in cottonwool.'

'Touché!' He smiled in recognition of his own barbed comment at her expense. The smile cut through her hostility, melting some submerged layer of ice. 'Tess, let's not wrangle—let's take as we find; start from here and now. Whatever we've been or done, we can enjoy each other's company while I'm here, can't we? I like to get along with the people I work with. It's so much simpler.'

Was that all it was, to him? Well, what more did she want it to be? 'That's okay, Josh. I think we understand each other.'

If only that was true, her mind taunted. She hardly even understood herself.

It was nearly four when they emerged from the restaurant. Tess wondered where the time had gone. Once they had steered the conversation away from those dangerous personal arenas it had seemed so keen to return to, it had ranged enjoyably over a variety of different topics. They had exchanged opinions, tastes and experiences. She had been surprised at the number of subjects they had found themselves agreeing vehemently about. And when they disagreed, it only added spice to their discussions.

Tess was thoroughly disconcerted. Men, as companions, had always fallen into two categories for her: the ones you could talk to, and the ones you had to fight off. Neither of them had ever tended to be very stimulating; but on the whole she preferred the first. With Joshua Mayer, it seemed, she had stumbled upon a rare example of the species: a man who was sensitive, clever and fun to be with—but with whom, all the time, there was that unfamiliar thread of tension which made you tingle and kept you on your toes. With this morning's aberration safely behind them, she found his company challenging and strangely fulfilling. As long as he didn't make any more such demands, she decided, they were going to get on fine. If it was an easy-going working relationship he was after, he certainly knew how to go about getting it.

'Like films?' he asked her now as they set off along the crowded pavement.

Tess hoped she was walking straight: the potent effects of the wine were still with her. 'Love them.'

'There's a good one on just down the hill—French—how about it? Should be a performance about five. That gives us time to walk off our lunch first.'

'I'd like that. Thanks.' Why not? She had nothing else particularly to do.

They wandered round the shops as the light slowly faded. He bought some fruit; and she bought a plaited loaf from a delicatessen. They stared into brightly-lit windows at unbelievably expensive clothes, shoes, jewellery and other consumer durables. No wonder Tess very rarely came up here, even though she lived so near; most of it was out of her league.

'These prices are astronomical,' he remarked, echoing her thoughts as usual. 'And Britain is supposed to be in a slump!'

'There are always some who remain untouched by such difficulties—and who can afford to live up here,' she told him pointedly.

'I consider convenience well worth paying for,' he countered. 'And yes,' he went on cheerfully, 'I *can* afford it. Why shouldn't I live where I like?' She wasn't quite sure exactly when, but he had taken her hand in his again.

'No reason at all,' she assured him.

* * *

The film was light and escapist: Tess's French was good enough for her to follow what was going on without the subtitles. The cinema, which she had often been to, was airy and comfortable. She felt acutely aware of the presence of the man next to her—and yet relaxed and distant, as if the events of the day had been happening to another person, and she had been watching them. Like the larger-than-life people and actions now filling the screen in front of her. Like a dream, from which she supposed she would wake up eventually. For the moment, though, she wouldn't mind if it went on a bit longer.

She yawned as they left the cinema, although it was only seven-thirty. Josh looked down at her. 'Tired?'

It was dark, and much chillier. She wound her scarf tighter round her neck. 'A bit. I'd better get home—I didn't bring a jacket.' She shivered.

'I've exhausted you,' he said contritely, 'one way and another.'

'No, really,' she protested. 'I was tired anyway. It's been a heavy week.'

'It certainly has.' Of course, he had had a part in that, too. She wondered whether he was going to invite her back to his flat. When he didn't, she hardly knew whether to feel relieved or disappointed. 'I'll run you home, Tess. You've had enough for one day, it seems to me.'

'I think I know when I've had enough,' she reproached him, finding a burst of her usual spirit.

'Okay, okay!' He backed off, holding up both hands in self-defence. 'I had your best interests at heart; I'm not after stealing your precious autonomy, Doc Hope.'

Tess flushed: of course he wasn't. She must learn not to be so touchy. He was quite considerate, really—even human. Eventually she might get used to being with a man who was both those things—as well as being so obviously, so powerfully . . . well, a man. 'Sorry,' she muttered. 'Didn't mean to bite your head off . . .'

He placed one long finger on her lips. 'Enough of that. Now,' he repeated, 'time to get you home.' And he marched her back to the car and drove her smoothly through the early evening traffic; back to her little house, and her river, and Fritz. Back to reality. She sighed.

He glanced at her. 'What is it, Tess? Have you enjoyed the afternoon?'

'I have,' she told him simply. 'Considering the inauspicious start, it's been great. Thanks, Josh.' It was amazing, the ease with which his name fell into place; this time yesterday, she would never have believed it possible.

'We must do it again some time.' He pulled up outside her house and switched off the ignition. They sat surrounded by a friendly, shadowy silence. Suddenly his proximity overwhelmed her; his presence filled up the confined space until her whole being was one mass of painful awareness of it. Her hand reached for the door handle.

'Wait, Tess.' The voice was low but commanding. She turned to meet his eyes—pools of deep grey in the dusk. 'I won't repeat this morning's episode, I promise—but don't rush off in quite such a hurry.'

'Would you like to come in for . . . coffee?' she croaked bravely.

He smiled. 'No, thanks. I appreciate it, but I have to get back.' She thought she detected that anxious look again, behind the smile; then it was gone. 'But I have time to take a proper leave of you,' he said softly.

He reached out then, and his hands were on her shoulders again—but gently, this time, pulling her towards him on the long front seat. She moved pliantly, easily, still as if in a dream. This time there was no bitter struggle; it was all so right, so simple, like a well-oiled machine—everything running exactly as it should.

Her mouth had only been waiting for the touch of his before it opened and came to life; her hands had been storing up instincts that would tell them to wind themselves round his neck, tangling their fingers in his vigorous dark hair. Her body was mysteriously ready, with no instruction from her, to press itself against his, arching and curving and pleading with his hands to run up and down the length of it, stroking and stoking it into a glowing flame which filled her consciousness, burning holes in all her preconceptions.

This time he was tender where he had been fierce before; gentle, where he had been harsh. This time her response was as total, as natural, as last time it had been negative. All thought forgotten, she returned his kisses—at first tentative, tasting, then deep and searching—with an equal passion.

It was Josh who pulled away at last, breaking the silence with a husky laugh. 'Couldn't let you go off with the taste of this morning still in your mouth!' That long finger traced her jawbone, coming to rest on her lips. 'Is it sore? Did I hurt you, Tess?'

'It's okay now.' Her voice was hardly more than a whisper. 'I didn't exactly enjoy it at the time, but . . .' it was worth it, she almost added.

'. . . but you've forgiven me now?' His hands framed her face with infinite care. 'I'm afraid it's all part of the same great dance. The dance of human nature . . . of my nature. Of male nature?' he suggested quizzically, a humorous glint in his eyes.

'Could be,' she confessed, with uncharacteristic docility.

'Anyway,' he took both her hands in his, 'it's over now. I promise it won't be like that again. It'll be like this—if you'll let it.' He kissed her cheek, her eyes, the tip of her nose, the corner of her mouth; and she had never in her life known anything so tantalising. She gasped, struggling to control the fluttering and clenching his actions had let loose inside her—their effect far more powerful than any amount of force could ever be. Try a little tenderness, the old song said: she could see why—it was the ultimate weapon in the battle of the sexes.

'Now,' suddenly brisk, Josh released her hands, sitting back to smile at her, 'I really do have to go. I have an appointment.'

On a Saturday evening? her mind taunted, grinding into action after its brief holiday. What sort of 'appointment' would that be? He reached over to open the door for her, and she got out, 'Thanks for the lunch, and everything,' she said, before closing it.

'Everything?' One eyebrow quirked; she could just make it out in the dim light.

'Nearly everything,' she modified.

'Don't thank me, Tess. I enjoyed it too. I'll see you Monday? We'll make a start on our syllabus together—in peace and harmony?'

'I'll do my best to make it peaceful and harmonious. As long as you don't argue too much,' she warned.

'I'll try not to,' he promised, with deceptive meekness. 'It takes two to argue, as well,' he reminded her gently, starting up the engine.

She walked through the gate and up the short front path, scrabbling in her bag for her keys. Reaching her door, she turned to wave—and he watched her disappear into the safe, familiar darkness of her silent house.

CHAPTER SIX

ON a grey Sunday afternoon early in November, Tess and her bicycle arrived on the doorstep of a Victorian terraced house—larger, shabbier, but in all other respects a recognisable relative of her own. The day was chilly and raw: she could see her breath steaming on the damp air, but her face and body glowed from energetic pedalling. She rang the bell on the peeling red front door.

Eventually it opened, and a small round face beamed up at her from the threshold. A straight, fair fringe fell into friendly light-blue eyes. A high, clear voice greeted her succinctly. 'Tess! You're late!'

'Hallo, Jamie. How's my friend?'

'I'm okay. We're making a bonfire—it's Guy Fawkes tomorrow.'

'I know. I'm sorry I'm late. Have I kept you waiting for tea?'

'Tea?' He frowned, puzzled. 'Oh no, Mum's been helping us. I don't think she's made any tea yet. Come in,' he invited politely, standing aside so that she could wheel her cycle into the wide cluttered hallway. 'Leave the bike . . . somewhere,' he instructed vaguely.

She leant it against the wall, along with assorted others—as well as push-chairs, pedal-cars, coats, toys—and, no doubt, last week's uneaten sandwiches. This home was not noted for its tidiness; but its warmth was tangible. Then she followed her small host into the kitchen, where the usual disorganised evidence of family life struck her in sharp contrast to her own ordered existence.

Jamie, the oldest of the three children, was already on his way out through the back door. 'Mum! Dad! It's Tess!' he shouted, running towards them.

Tess looked out of the kitchen window. The whole family was busy at the bottom of the long narrow garden, collecting wood and stacking it into a pile. Tim—tall and thin, bearded, balding, bespectacled—issued instructions while he sawed up the biggest pieces. The two little girls, Emma and Lucy, scurried helpfully about clutching bundles of twigs. Hilary had obviously been arranging their offerings into a combustible shape, with her son's help. She and Tim were both dressed in ancient flared jeans and thick guernsey sweaters. They looked up now, grinning and waving at Tess.

'I'll come and join you!' she shouted, waving back.

'No, stay there,' Hilary called. 'I've got to come in and start the tea.'

Making sure Jamie knew his job, she left her family and squelched up the muddy path to the back door, where she took off her boots, left them outside and appeared in the warm kitchen in her socks, her cheeks bright red.

'Hallo, Tess. Sorry not to be here to greet you properly. Important family commitment, as you saw.'

'I certainly did. You must let me help.'

Hilary washed her hands, moving aside a few piles of dirty crockery in the sink first. 'No, we've finished really. They'll all be glad to come in soon—it's already getting dark.'

'Awful, isn't it? Getting dark so early?' How English they were, Tess found herself reflecting, with their preoccupations about the weather and the seasons. 'Soon be Christmas,' she remarked cheerfully.

Hilary shuddered, drying her hands on a towel that had seen cleaner days. 'Do you *mind*? Christmas indeed! This term's hardly under way!'

'Don't you believe it,' returned Tess darkly, her hands in the deep pockets of her cord trousers as she leaned against the table. 'It'll be here before you can say holly.'

Hilary made a face at her. 'Thanks for nothing!' She smiled, glancing closely at her friend for the first time. 'And how are things with *you*, Dr Hope? It seems a long time since I've had you to myself . . . apart from snatched moments in our wonderful canteen, and they hardly count.'

'I know—I've been . . . rather busy,' Tess explained, her brown eyes suddenly intent upon the toes of her leather boots.

'So I gathered.' Hilary cleared a space among the débris, produced a loaf and several packets of crumpets and began to collect together the ingredients of the afternoon tea to which Tess had originally been invited. 'Every time I see you, you're a sort of . . . radiant blur,' she accused, rummaging in the fridge for the butter. 'I had to phone three times before I found you at home. What is this—the new socialite edition? Whatever happened to the girl who thrived on her own company and was proud to stay at home marking essays and improving her already powerful mind?'

Tess grinned at this total exaggeration. 'I was hardly the recluse you make me out to be. Not quite as intellectual as that. But I admit I've been a bit . . . difficult to pin down lately. Here,' she added, rolling up her sleeves and going over to the sink. 'Let me do all this washing-up while you get the tea. You can't move among all this mess, surely?'

'Thanks.' Hilary took the implied criticism of her housekeeping habits in the spirit it had been offered.

Both women were quite used to each other's different approaches to life by now: their relationship was all the better for it. 'Tim usually does all that after lunch, but today we were all keen to get out there and start the bonfire . . . you know how it is.'

Tess smiled at her. 'Of course I do. It's great. I'm glad to have something useful to do, anyway—you know me.' She ran a bowlful of hot water and attacked the first stack of greasy plates with gusto. Through the window she could see Tim and the children, still engrossed in their various tasks in the fading light.

'I know you.' Hilary put the first batch of crumpets under the grill. 'At least, I thought I did—I'm beginning to wonder.' She opened a tin to get a fruit cake out and ease it on to a plate. 'Latest developments seem to suggest I don't know you as well as I thought I did.'

'How do you mean?' Tess glanced over her shoulder, elbow-deep in suds. Her dark brows were raised into her curls, all bewildered innocence.

'How do I mean?' Hilary echoed satirically. 'You know very well what I'm talking about, Tess. But,' she sniffed, slicing the loaf viciously, 'you don't have to tell me if you don't want to. I'm only your best friend, that's all. Or I thought I was,' she added in an offended tone.

'But Hil . . .' Tess glanced round again, her expression anxious this time. Hilary was grinning broadly, so she grinned back. 'It's not like that at all. I've had a lot on my mind—first this flood in my cellar, then it's been as much as I could handle, getting this new course under way and everything . . .'

'Ah yes; the new course.' Hilary began spreading butter on to crumpets. 'How's it going? Not too badly, from all I've heard?'

'What have you heard?' Tess scrubbed hard at a particularly grimy glass.

'Well, the students are pleased. Prof Slocombe's delighted. Bill Jones was saying to me on Friday that you and the great Professor Mayer appear to be . . . getting along reasonably well.' She was, Tess knew, picking her words with extreme care. 'Do I understand,' she went on more directly, 'that the situation isn't turning out to be quite so difficult or threatening as you originally expected? That you're managing to conduct yourselves like mature, intelligent people after all? The way you were at each other's throats, I feared for both your skins. Especially yours, Tess.' A serious note had crept into her voice. 'He's an experienced, tough man, you know. A fighter—it's easy to see that. I was afraid . . .'

'I'd be no match for him? I know, Hil . . . you did warn me, remember? I took in your well-chosen words. I always listen to my wise Auntie Hil, don't I?'

'You listen,' her friend agreed, 'but then you go off and do what you were about to do anyway. Still,' she shrugged, 'I can't do more than warn you.'

'It's okay.' Tess turned round to face her, the spongemop still in one hand. 'Don't worry, Hil, I know what I'm doing . . . I think. And if I don't,' she went on, her expression suddenly lighting up with an incandescent glow she could no longer hide, 'I don't care. It's too late to care. I'm in it now, up to the neck,' she confessed, eyes bright, lips trembling a little. 'Over the top of my head,' she corrected ruefully.

Hilary stared at her, knife poised in mid-air. 'Like that, is it?' Head on one side, she perused her friend thoughtfully. 'I wondered if it might be. Are you going to tell me about it, Tess—I mean really tell me?' She looked through the window. 'Before the hordes come in for their tea—which won't be very long now, by the look of it.'

'There's not much to tell, Hil.' Tess turned back to the

sink and went on washing up, glad to have something to occupy her hands while she talked. She had known Hilary would raise this question, and she had been prepared to talk about it—but even so, it wasn't easy. For one thing, no suitable words existed in the English language, as far as she knew (and she had a doctorate in the subject) to express the way she felt . . . to describe what was going on. 'I can't even tell you quite how it happened.'

'How what happened?' Hilary enquired sharply.

'Give me a chance!' Tess cleared her throat. 'How it started. One moment we were—as you said—at each other's throats. I hated him, and all he stood for—for barging in and taking over my course, and then trying to take me over as well . . .'

'And just how,' Hilary interrupted, 'did he do that? This gets more interesting every minute.'

'How do you think?' There was no point in prevaricating: Hilary knew perfectly well what she was talking about. 'He thought I was an . . . easy target. He came round to the house to see me—some excuse about my river . . .'

'Oh yes,' Hilary remembered. 'How *is* your river?'

'Much the same—just sort of . . . there. Anyway, he's interested in the Fleet and other underground streams in London, so he came to see mine. Then we went to the Heath to take a look at the rest of it. Then we had a meal.' It sounded so simple, put like that.

'And?' Hilary encouraged, glued to her every syllable.

'Well, at first he got the wrong idea about me. He . . . tried it on. But then I made it clear I wasn't . . .'

'That sort of girl?' suggested Hilary drily.

'I suppose so.' Tess wondered briefly whether Josh had been right, after all—but it was too late to look back now. That was two weeks ago: a lot of water had, as it were, flowed under the bridge since then. 'He became very sweet and charming after that. Quite apologetic. Suddenly,' she admitted, with difficulty, 'it was easy to stop being so hostile. We had a really nice afternoon together, and since then we've been out quite a few times. And the course is working out well, yes—because we get on well. We seem to have the same way of going about things. I've even enjoyed it,' she declared, defying Hilary to laugh at her for this change of heart.

But Hilary wasn't laughing. 'Where have you been out to?' she pressed, chopping up a cucumber. 'You mean, evenings—that sort of thing?'

'Yes, evenings. And last weekend we spent some time together. We've been to the cinema and the theatre—once to the West End, and once to a fringe show. To two meals, and . . . let me see . . . a rock concert.'

'A rock concert?' Hilary's eyebrows shot up. 'That doesn't sound like your scene at all. I've never met the man yet who could get you to one of those!'

'True—but you have now. Josh is a man of catholic tastes. He likes all kinds of music. He says I need educating . . . my horizons broadening.'

'Josh, is it?' Hilary's eyes gleamed in sardonic delight.

'Well, what do you expect me to call him? Professor? We have a working relationship,' Tess reminded her heatedly.

'Of course, of course. What else, indeed?' Hilary soothed. 'Go on.'

'Go on with what?' Tess started on the last pan.

'Telling me all about it.'

'There isn't much more. We've been out; we've worked together. It seems to be working out okay. That's it.'

Judging by the warmth in her friend's normally cool

features, 'that' was far from being 'it'; but Hilary knew better than to push hard at a moment like this. 'I'm glad, Tess,' she said gently. 'You deserved it.'

'Deserved what?' Tess knew she sounded touchy, but it wasn't easy, giving up an image of yourself which you had fostered for so many careful years.

'You know what I mean.' Hilary tried again. 'You don't always think very highly of our male associates, or men in general. You haven't exactly . . . hit it off with any particular one yet, as I recall. Not that I blame you,' she went on hastily. 'If Tim and I hadn't got together at the ridiculously tender age we did, I often think I'd have been just the same as you. As it is . . .' there was tenderness in her eyes as she stared through the window again at her family, 'I wouldn't have missed it for anything; but it's different for you, Tess—keeping your independence all these years. Hanging on to it as if it's the last friend you've got.'

'Have I really seemed like that?' Tess swung round, surprised.

'In a way. I don't blame you—that's what I'm saying.'

'I haven't given up my independence,' Tess pointed out, 'just because I've temporarily let someone into my life. I mean, just because I've been out with them a few times . . .' she turned back to scouring her pan.

'Never let it be said.' Hilary filled the kettle. 'And is that all you've done—gone out? You haven't . . . stayed in as well?' This was a delicate question, and she knew it; but somehow she sensed it needed to be asked. Not that she was probing, of course—but Tess managed to give the impression she wanted to talk, even when she was being cagey.

'Stayed in?' Tess frowned, then blushed. 'Oh, I see what you mean. Well, not really . . . he came to supper once. That was nice.' She smiled at the recent memory:

Josh had eaten her best efforts at goulash with every sign of enjoyment. But then he had had to leave early—to get back, he said, to keep to a previous arrangement, and she had barely been able to disguise her disappointment. 'To tell you the truth, Hil . . .' suddenly overcome with a need for honesty, she turned back to face her friend, 'we haven't been alone together much, since that first morning . . . he'll hardly ever come in, and he never asks me back to his flat. I've never seen it. I don't even know exactly where it is. He's told me he isn't married, and I believe him, but that's all I know . . . and he does seem to rush off after our times together, but from the way he behaves towards me, I'm sure he was telling me the truth.' She subsided, her gaze dropping.

'How does he behave?' Hilary asked quietly.

'Oh—attentive, caring. He seems interested in me—really interested, you know.' She still couldn't lift her eyes; it wasn't easy, this sort of conversation, she thought wistfully.

But Hilary was doing her best to make it as easy as possible. 'Interested—how? Sexually? Emotionally?' she suggested.

'He made it clear right from the start that it was . . . the first. Then, when I reacted very negatively, he changed, and ever since then he's been . . . gentle, careful. Undemanding. Holding back.' She sighed. 'As if I was made of glass, almost,' she reflected, half to herself. 'But still definitely interested. You know what I mean?'

Hilary nodded. 'Of course. Sounds serious to me,' she said slowly. 'A man like that—he could have women falling over themselves . . .'

'And frequently does,' Tess interjected grimly. 'He's made that perfectly clear, on more than one occasion.'

'Well then, there's no way he'd bother with anyone

who doesn't. Not unless he was interested,' Hilary confirmed. 'Not in my experience.'

'That's what I thought,' said Tess, smiling—allowing her persistent happiness to break through again. 'If you really want to know, Hil . . .' she confided.

'I want to know.' Hilary returned the smile.

'. . . the way I feel now, I wouldn't mind if he did—you know—if he stopped holding back on me.' Tess drew a deep breath. 'If he tried again, the way he did at first. I wasn't ready then—I was taken by surprise. But now . . . I enjoy his company, as it is, but I could take more. Now that I feel this way.' She knew the colour was rising in her cheeks, but she wasn't giving up, having got this far. Telling the truth to Hilary, it was the first time she had really confessed it to herself. 'I'm not sure how to let him know. I've never had this problem before, you see.'

'No, you haven't been noted for your tendency to lead men on, Tess.' Hilary began laying the table. 'Fighting men off has been more your style, from what you've always told me.'

'Exactly. So I feel a bit . . . stuck.' Tess sighed again. 'Hilary, it's only been a fortnight, and I don't really know him; but I've never felt this way before—about anyone.' There was a tremor in her voice which she couldn't control. 'Whatever it is, I don't suppose it'll last, on either side—but at least now I know I *can* feel something for a man. I was beginning to be afraid . . .'

'You'd die an old maid?' Hilary teased.

'I still might, at this rate,' Tess concluded gloomily.

Hilary stopped what she was doing and leaned on the table, arms folded. She looked Tess straight in the eye. 'I always suspected,' she said, 'that when you finally fell, Tess Hope, you'd fall the whole way. Hook, line and sinker. You've never been one to do things by halves,' she pointed out. 'In a way you've had this coming: I felt the vibes between you, that first time we met him. You could have cut them with a knife. I had a feeling it was only a matter of time.'

'Did you really?' Tess was genuinely amazed. 'But I hated him! He said something similar himself—about the messages between us—that first Saturday. I was appalled.'

'You were naïve,' Hilary told her candidly. 'One level of you was unaware of what the other was feeling—or saying.'

'That's just what he said,' Tess mused. 'I was furious.'

'There you are, you see? Auntie Hil knows about these things.'

They exchanged brief smiles. Tess felt better, having put that much into words. It didn't make the situation any clearer, but at least she had heard herself saying them. 'I know. Wise old Auntie Hil!'

'Not so much of the old!' Tim and the children were walking slowly up the garden; it was nearly dark. The kettle boiled and whistled through the peaceful London evening. In a spontaneous gesture, Hilary stepped towards Tess and took one hand in her own. 'Don't worry,' she said softly. 'Just let it work itself out. Being in love is always painful, even when it's wonderful. But it's always worth it, in the end.' She glanced through the window as the shadowy form of her husband approached, one child hanging on to each arm. 'However it pans out.' Just for a moment, her eyes were far away.

Suddenly Tess understood her friend very well. 'Tim hasn't been the only man in your life, has he?' she challenged on an impulse.

'No. He was the first; I know now he'll be the last. He's always been the important one—but I'm only human, and female, and vulnerable . . . you know.'

Tess nodded. 'Are you still in love with him, now?' she asked, almost on a whisper.

'Sure—why not?' The other woman grinned. 'We should all be in love. It makes life much more exciting.'

'Is that what I am?' Tess persisted, her voice low but intense. 'In love?'

Hilary stared closely into her face. 'I should say,' she replied firmly, 'that there isn't a jot of doubt about that. Congratulations.' She patted Tess on the arm, releasing her as she prepared to greet her family, now noisily pulling off their muddy boots at the door. 'Welcome to the human race.'

'Is tea ready?' an assortment of voices, deep and squeaky, demanded. 'We're starving!'

The next day Tess was due to give her weekly lecture to the General Arts students, and Professor Slocombe had asked whether she minded if Joshua Mayer sat in on the hour so that he could see how she was approaching the subject. At first she had hated the idea; but now that they had become so easy with each other she decided it wouldn't be so bad.

He arrived when she was well under way, flashed her a conspiratorial wink and made his way quietly to the back of the room, where he sat for the rest of the time, his dark brows furrowed in concentration. Occasionally he made a note, but more often he just sat, listening intently to everything she said. She tried to avoid his eye, but it was impossible not to glance up once in a while and catch it: her heart lurched in a highly unprofessional manner every time she glimpsed that quizzical half-smile across the heads between them.

Afterwards, when she had answered the few inevitable questions that come up at the end of a lively lecture, and all the students had finally shuffled out of the hall, he got up and came to join her at the desk. 'Great stuff,' he told her enthusiastically.

She looked up at him sharply. Was he being satirical? Even now she found it hard, sometimes, to be quite sure. 'Really?'

'Really. I mean it. You're a great little speaker, Doc Hope. You're in charge of your audience—just as you're in charge of yourself.'

In charge of herself? In his company that was the last thing she felt—she must be doing a better cover-up job than she thought. 'Glad you approved, Professor,' she said lightly.

'I approve of most things about you, Tess, as you well know.' She clenched, inwardly, at the intimacy in his tone. 'I expected no less of you. You're a professional to your fingertips. You were quite right to want to guard your hard-won reputation in your field. I'm glad we didn't have to take any of it away from you. Whatever I can do will only enhance an already brilliantly devised course.'

There was little to be said in reply to that. Tess gathered up her notes, reddening under his direct gaze. 'Thanks, Josh. So you think I should carry on with the lectures just as I am?'

'Definitely. Don't change a thing. Don't change anything about yourself. You're great the way you are.'

She looked him straight in the eye. 'You're teasing me.' She drew herself up, squaring her shoulders. 'I don't need buttering up, you know. I've got over all that hostility I was suffering from. I know now that you're not out to seize my students from under my nose, so there's no need for such flattery.'

'Flattery?' His tone and expression were deeply offended. 'I don't go in for flattery, my dear Tess. I say what I mean—and not a syllable more. I had hoped you appreciated that by now.' He flicked a glance at his watch. 'Got to go and report to our colleague, Professor Slocombe. I shall assure him that we have the whole thing in hand. Shall I?'

'Of course.'

'We have, haven't we, Tess? Got this thing in hand?'

They walked to the door together and he opened it for her to go through. 'Sure—why not?' She was well aware of his double meaning; but this was a Monday morning. There was a time and a place, her tone suggested, for everything.

He grinned. 'Before you rush off to whatever fortunate class awaits you, Dr Hope . . .'

She turned to face him. 'Yes, Professor Mayer?'

'I've secured two tickets to a concert this evening. Would you consider accompanying me? I know it's short notice, but they were returns—I didn't know until this morning.'

'A concert? Where? What?'

'Royal Festival Hall—Brahms and Franck, the Royal Philharmonic. More your line, I think,' he added, 'than the previous musical soirée I subjected you to.' His tone was serious, but there was a wry twist to his mouth.

'I liked it,' Tess protested; and, surprisingly, it was true. The atmosphere had reached her: the insistent beat of the band, the noisy enjoyment of the audience, her acute awareness of her companion—they had all combined to make the evening one of the most exciting she had ever spent. She was still regretting the fact that he'd had to leave her on her doorstep and rush away at the end of it.

'In your way, I think you really did,' he acknowledged, black brows knitting over hooked nose as he recalled her amazed reaction to the scene. 'Anyway, how about tonight?'

She thought quickly. It wasn't like her to be at some-one's beck and call, not even his, but this sounded too good to miss. Her favourite composer, Brahms; and a top orchestra in a top concert hall. And Josh's company for a whole evening. She made up her mind. 'I'll come—thanks.' Her mouth curved, her eyes brightened. 'I'll look forward to it. Where shall I meet you?'

'I'll pick you up. Seven,' he ordered. 'We'll eat after,' he added as she turned to leave. 'Okay?'

'Okay.' He was already striding off down the corridor, broad back receding into the distance. Tess stared after it, swallowing hard to fight down the alarming emotions the sight of it churned up inside her. Eat afterwards! That was the first time he had issued such an invitation— or rather, she amended mentally, an instruction; usually he was in too much of a hurry to get home. As she had confided to Hilary, it puzzled her; but she tried not to think about it too hard.

She was ready at seven in a plain silk shirt and long, swirling black skirt, with her tall grey suede boots. Josh opened the car door for her, and leaned over to kiss her lightly on the cheek. 'Hi, Tess. You're looking gorgeous.' He started up the engine.

'You don't look so bad yourself.' She hardly recog-nised the person making this bold statement; but she meant it. He was wearing a casual dark close-fitting suit, and looked groomed and distinguished. Only the black mane, refusing to be tamed, crowned the carved fea-tures with its usual vigorous disorder. She was aware that her physical responses to him were growing stronger than ever, and held herself tense, keeping them carefully hidden.

But Josh was still all chivalry and small attentions: it was as if he had never even hinted at that darker, more passionate level of communication between them. One hand took hers as they walked from the car park, long fingers winding themselves subtly through hers so that she had to suppress a gasp. Later, in the interval, when they went to find a drink at the bar, the same hand cupped her elbow with smooth, nonchalant confidence, guiding her skilfully through the milling crowds in the foyer. Apart from those moments, he never touched her; and his conversation remained impersonal and undemanding.

She always enjoyed visiting this great concert hall, with its stretches of simple, natural wood; its vast, spreading organ pipes and its beautiful acoustic. The orchestra played superbly: the Fourth Symphony by Brahms was one of her favourite pieces and she let it wash over her, sensing the relief as she allowed her mind and body to relax for once. After the interval, the Franck Symphony—which she didn't know well—was equally soothing and involving. She succeeded in switching off her mind as effectively as she ever did—which was just as well, because once it was given free rein there was no knowing what it might start to harangue her about.

Afterwards they leaned over the wall of the Embankment and gazed at the night-time Thames, with its thousands of reflected lights; at Hungerford and Waterloo Bridges, and all the buildings floodlit on both banks; and at the craft of all shapes and sizes which chugged and glided down the river, even at this hour. Police launches, goods barges . . . even a brightly-lit pleasure boat full of sybaritic revellers who waved and shouted to them as they passed.

There was a sharp breeze. Tess drew her coat tighter round her, shivering. At once Josh's arm was about her shoulders, pulling her into the warmth of his own body. 'Don't be cold, Tess. It's so beautiful, I thought we should pay our respects to it.'

'Of course we should. I always do, when I come down here. I'm fine, really.'

'Are you, Tess? Are you really all right?'

She looked at him, surprised. 'Of course. Why shouldn't I be?'

His face was very close to hers. 'No reason. Just as long as you are. I like being with you very much, Tess—you know that, don't you?'

Before she could reply that the feeling was mutual, he was kissing her—very gently but very thoroughly; and the lights spun and reeled so that she had to shut her eyes until the world decided to keep still again. How was it that he made her feel—and behave—like a lovesick adolescent . . . was it, perhaps, because she had never really *had* a lovesick adolescence? Had she really had it coming to her all these years, as Hilary had so wisely put it?

Josh released her before the kiss could deepen into anything alarming—or, at least, before he thought it could. Her own response to it was quite alarming enough. Then they walked slowly together, eastwards as far as the National Theatre—towards the great, shining dome of St Paul's, keeping its ancient watch over the City. Turning, they strolled back, past the three concert halls again and the National Theatre—and there, further up ahead of them, the face of Big Ben stood out on the skyline, guarding the Houses of Parliament.

'Rivers,' Josh remarked lazily, his arm squeezing her shoulders. 'We seem destined to find ourselves in their company.'

'At least this one's open and above ground,' she pointed out, as firmly as possible, 'and not hidden away out of sight in a pipe.'

'Our friend the Fleet was above ground once,' he reminded her, 'just like this.'

He took her to a small Spanish restaurant in Soho, and they ate paella and syllabub while a soulful guitarist hovered round their table. Tess had always considered such entertainment intrusive; but now she entered into the spirit of the occasion, laughing and blushing when their serenader presented her solemnly with a red rose, which she stuck behind her ear amongst her dark curls.

'Beautiful, *señorita*,' he pronounced with a deep sigh.

'Beautiful,' echoed Josh, with hardly a hint of a smile; and she almost believed them.

She was half asleep when the yellow Renault drew smoothly up outside her front door. It had been a very busy day at college; and then there were the emotional effects of the music, followed by the rich food and plentiful wine . . . her head was suddenly a pleasant haze, through which coherent thought was struggling to emerge. She let it struggle: she had had enough coherent thought, she decided, to last a lifetime.

'Coming in,' she suggested, as usual and without much hope, 'for a coffee?'

'Sure,' Josh agreed at once.

She sat up straight. 'What did you say?'

'I said sure. Why?' he teased. 'Didn't really mean it? Want to withdraw your kind invitation?'

'Of course not!' She stifled a hiccup. 'I invited you in, and I meant it. It's just that . . . you don't . . .'

'I don't have to leave so early tonight—except that it's another working day tomorrow for us both. I'd be glad to accept a cup of your excellent coffee, if it's really on offer.' He flashed her a sidelong grin in the dimness of the car. 'You look as though you could do with a cup yourself.'

Tess wasn't arguing with that. She searched in her bag for her keys, and then she walked ahead of him up the path and unlocked the door. Fritz greeted them with cries of eager complaint, and she picked him up and hugged him. 'Okay, okay,' she told him, 'you'll get fed. Don't panic!'

Josh watched sardonically. 'That cat,' he declared, 'gets more attention than any animal has a right to expect. More than most children—or men,' he accused, and his tone was not entirely frivolous.

Tess put the cat down. 'Why not? I don't have a child—or a man,' she pointed out. 'Anyway, he gives as good as he gets—don't you, Fritz?' Fritz purred in loud agreement: it was all give, give, give, he seemed to say—his life was one long-suffering martyrdom. 'See?' she said, turning to Josh, who had gone very quiet as he watched her stroking her pet.

'Sure, Tess.' His voice was very soft; his eyes fixed on the rhythmic movements of her hand on the sleek fur. She looked away.

'Make yourself comfortable in there,' she said, 'while I get the coffee.'

Five minutes later she appeared in the sitting room, carrying a tray on which were the pot, two mugs, milk and sugar—leaving Fritz to attack his bowl in the kitchen as if his life depended on it. Josh was sprawled on the thick rug, investigating the lower shelves of her book-cases. He had drawn the heavy orange curtains over the bay window, and lit one small lamp: the room was envelopingly warm and welcoming, just as she had planned it, with its oatmeal furniture and carpets, and the touches of brown and orange here and there.

She set the tray down on the low coffee table and knelt beside it. 'Black?'

'Please. You know how I like it—strong, black, tasty, like you make it.' He went on inspecting her library. 'I see you go for Doris Lessing?'

'I think she's wonderful, don't you?'

'I guess so. Very mystic.'

'Not her earlier books,' Tess began, pouring his coffee and leaning over to hand it to him. 'They're quite different. They . . .'

Josh moved towards her in order to take it. Their hands touched, and seemed welded together. Her gaze drew itself up to lock with his. In that endless moment, an overflowing tension broke free and pulled them into its force field. It was very quiet in the room.

She cleared her throat. 'Shall I put some music on?' she suggested desperately, abandoning her critique of Doris Lessing's earlier works.

He put his coffee down carefully on the lowest shelf behind him. 'Not for a minute, Tess. Stay here—don't go.'

His hand came out to grab hers before she could retreat; warm, determined, pulling her inexorably across the rug until she was near enough for him to take her in his arms. 'I'm not going anywhere,' she heard herself murmuring faintly, as she let herself be gathered up—weightless, thoughtless—in that powerful embrace. Everything pointed in one direction: there was no fight in her—only acceptance, and longing, and that profound, eternal knowledge that this was what she was for . . . this was what she had always wanted. And hadn't she always—surely, surely—wanted it from this man?

Now his face was buried in her hair; his lips moving against her neck, her cheeks, her eyes. The gentle hands had mysteriously transformed themselves again into those fiercely demanding creatures she had met once before, gripping her upper arms as if they wanted to break them in two. 'Tess,' he whispered. 'Tess.' His voice was a soft groan, at the back of his throat. 'I can't keep up this pretence any longer. I want you—can't you see, I want you, more than anything in the world. I've got to have you . . .'

His lips had found hers, and the words merged into actions—forcing them apart, plundering deeply, desperately into their inner softness. Tess gave, and gave—pushed back under his weight until she lay on the rug and he leaned over her; and still she gave, and still he demanded more, until she knew there was no more to be given in a simple kiss. Her body, her whole being, screamed that there was no more room for pretence. He was right.

'Josh.' Her own voice was strange—thick, husky. 'Josh.' She broke away from his hungry mouth to speak his name on a gasp. 'Please!'

What was she pleading for? Did she know? Whatever it was, he knew; and suddenly he was calm, waiting—smothering her face and neck with soft, light kisses until she no longer knew what was happening, except that everything in her ached with the love and longing he had awakened there. She knew only that this man must have what she could give. That he would have it; and that he would have it now.

Understanding that, he became gentle, his caresses more subtle than ever. His mouth teased and tantalised hers as his hands found a way past the barrier of her silk shirt to her breasts, the long fingers stroking them into urgent life. Then his lips moved down to take over, nibbling and sucking until she cried out, arching against him. It was too late to stop now. Too late—too late. She belonged to him; she was all his.

His own urgency was growing, yet he took his time. Tenderly, surely, expertly, he explored and reassured her, uncovering and discovering every sensitive nerve, each secret place. Her own hands, untaught and yet somehow wise, guided and welcomed his—touching him, too, as if they did it every day . . . as if they had minds of their own, far cleverer than the one which had always ruled her actions before.

When at last she could bear it no longer, she implored him to take her; and he took her; and it was the only possible way ahead. She heard herself, from a great distance, call out his name once; and then there was nothing but that need, that overwhelming need—swelling, terrible and wonderful, until it filled every corner of her consciousness and all she could do was cry out loud and cling to him while the kaleidoscope shattered and a million colours cascaded through her.

Then she lay in his arms, her face, wet with her own tears, pressed into his neck; calm and full of a new understanding which told her that nothing in her life would ever be the same again. The silence settled itself around them. Josh breathed deeply, steadily against her. Was he asleep? Cautiously she opened an eye, moved away so that she could look up into his face.

He wasn't asleep. He was looking down at her with an expression of acute, almost painful tenderness that made her heart sing. He smiled, just slightly, and his arms tightened around her.

'Josh?'

'Tess?'

She looked down, burying her head in the warmth of his arm, unable to meet that steady, penetrating gaze.

'Tess?' he said again. One hand cupped her chin, forcing her face to turn up to his. 'Are you all right?'

'Of course I am.' She smiled, straight into his eyes. 'I'm fine.'

'You're fine,' he echoed, drawing her close again with a sigh. 'Tess Hope, fine is exactly what you are!'

Their coffee congealed in its mugs—unwanted, ignored. Fritz padded in from the kitchen and came over to join them, much impressed with this friendly huddle of human bodies. For creatures with such a miserable lack of fur, he reflected, it was amazing how much useful heat they could generate between them.

CHAPTER SEVEN

THE bus jolted and swayed its way through familiar packed streets—closely following the underground route of the Fleet, as Tess now knew. Sitting at the front of the top deck—on the seat she had always liked best, ever since she was a little girl—she hardly noticed the rough ride, or even the fumes from other passengers' cigarettes, which usually choked her. The way she felt, she might as well have been riding on Cloud Nine rather than at the mercy of London Transport. The grey, grimy buildings seemed friendlier than usual; the conductor managed a cheerful smile. It wasn't even raining. All in all, she thought, the world wasn't such a bad old place.

Still, she had to admit to being a bit weary. By the time Josh had kissed her tenderly one last time, got dressed and let himself out of the house—leaving Fritz and Tess in a warm huddle on the soft rug—it was well into the small hours. She hadn't bothered to look at a clock: she had crept up to her bedroom, and the rosy glow he had left had trailed up there with her. It had climbed into the small single bed with her, and stayed with her as she fell into a deep dreamless sleep.

It was still with her this morning—clinging round her, suffusing everything with its warmth. Really, she was behaving like a lovesick schoolgirl; but it was wonderful. When she thought of all the years she had missed out on this feeling, she realised she had a good bit of catching up to do. It was a pity Josh Mayer appeared to be the only man on earth who could achieve such results . . . but then why was it a pity? He was here; he had been only too willing to achieve them. There was no reason, as far as she could see, why he shouldn't go on achieving them—for the moment, at least. And the moment was what mattered—just this once; just for a change.

Not that her mind wasn't busy, as always, pushing through her euphoria with its own sensible messages. He was only here temporarily, it reminded her; and she still knew so little about him. Why, for instance, it demanded, had he been so determined to go home last night? It wouldn't have made much difference, after all, if he had stayed the last few hours till morning. She had fallen asleep in his arms, right there on the rug—she had no idea how long for; and the next thing she knew, he was waking her with light lingering kisses on her face, neck and breasts. Her brown eyes had flickered open to look up into his grey ones, overflowing with love for him.

'Josh?'

'Little Tess. I have to go—I'm sorry.'

'Go?' She struggled to sit up, her hair a tangled mass of curls. The room looked the same, but different. Everything felt the same, but different. 'Why?'

'It's very late, and I have a lot to do tomorrow.'

'But you can sleep here. Don't go, Josh,' she had implored.

'I must.' He had laid a finger on her lips. 'I don't want to, but I must. I shall see you again, very soon.'

She had lain back then; and the new, wanton Tess had stretched out her white arms to him, wrapping them round his neck, pulling him close to her until he groaned and his kisses became passionate again. 'Stay,' she had murmured.

'Brazen lady,' he had muttered, against her mouth; and stayed—just a while longer.

But he had gone later, when there were not many hours left of the night. Tess had watched him go, through half-closed eyes; but she had said nothing. There was nothing more to say. Words had become suddenly redundant.

This morning, however, they all piled back into her head. Why shouldn't he have stayed the rest of the night? Her bed might be small, but they could have squeezed into it—or slept right where they were, on the cosy rug. He could even have used her spare room if he needed his sleep that badly, she reflected wryly.

And then again, her mind pressed relentlessly on: what had got into her, letting a thing like that happen at all, especially without being prepared? Tess Hope, who was always so practical, so reliable—giving way to the ultimate instinct; becoming nothing but a mass of irrational emotion? Just suppose, the voice harped on at the back of her mind, she were to find herself pregnant as a result of last night? What would she feel like then, for God's sake? Hadn't she always sworn she'd never let it take her unawares, when it finally happened?

But, her heart replied, that was what had made it so special—the fact that it had been so completely unexpected. Neither of them had been planning it, that much was obvious; both of them had been totally taken by surprise at the way the evening had ended. She could tell that, from the way Josh had behaved. She would have expected a man like that—dominant, experienced—to be ready for anything, one jump ahead; but he had taken the gift she had offered him like a drowning man clutching at a raft. All his potent strength had poured itself into a powerful need for her, a craving which only possession of her could satisfy. She understood, because it had been the same for her.

Whatever happened now, she wasn't going to regret it: even in the cold light of day, it felt much too . . . right. Her mind could come up with as many dire warnings as it liked; it wasn't going to succeed in shattering her new cocoon of happiness—not this time.

Tuesday was Josh's day for going about his researches outside the College, so she knew she wouldn't see him today. But he was there with her all the time, somewhere, hovering at the back of her consciousness, a warm presence, wherever she went. If Hilary noticed an unusual abstractedness in her friend when they met briefly in the canteen, or if her students remarked on her air of dreamy lightheartedness, they all kept their observations to themselves.

She thought Josh might phone her that evening; but he didn't. Too busy out and about, poking into some old river or other, she thought fondly. Probably got back late and didn't want to disturb her, knowing she'd be tired. She was, too; after a long hot soak in a deep bath she put herself to bed very early with a light novel and Joan Armatrading on her portable cassette player.

She knew she would see him the next day. The two of them always got together with Bill Jones on a Wednesday to plan the next sessions in their course. But he did not turn up. Naturally, she was surprised and disappointed—but she and Bill managed it perfectly well on their own. Josh had set the wheels in motion with inspired efficiency; now it was really up to them.

In the afternoon she sat in her room and immersed herself in work, trying to fight thoughts of Josh away from their constant attack on her concentration. Trying, but not succeeding. A light tap on her door was enough to make her heart leap, her stomach clench. What was the point of pretending she wasn't waiting for him, all the time—just living for the moment when she'd see him again?

'Come in,' she called, as nonchalantly as possible.

The door opened, and she found herself confronting

Professor Slocombe's bifocals round the edge of it. 'Tess? Have you got a minute?'

'Of course.' She smiled at him, attempting not to wear her disappointment on her sleeve. 'Please come in.' She took off her reading glasses and held them in one hand, in a characteristic gesture.

'Hard at it, I see.' He sat opposite her, glancing approvingly at her pile of books. 'I just wanted to tell you how pleased we all are—the Board is—with the way things are working out. You have shown a most mature degree of co-operation, my dear, in this matter of the—er—new course . . .'

'I've enjoyed it, Professor,' she assured him honestly. Little did he know how much . . . or why! 'I'm sorry my initial reaction was so negative; but I'm sure you understood . . .'

'Yes, yes, of course—perfectly,' he interrupted earnestly. 'You overcame it in the most masterful manner, if I may use the—er—term,' he added with a dry stab at humour.

'You may,' Tess allowed graciously. She was less touchy, these days, on the subject of male chauvinism than she had once been, for some reason.

'As I say, we are all delighted with progress. The students are happy—and therefore Dr Jones is happy. If you and Professor Mayer are also happy . . .'

'I think we are,' she told him solemnly.

'Good, good. He's not such a difficult—er—person to work with, is he? Quite—er—amenable, once you get to know him?' he enquired, leaning forward and linking bony fingers together on her desk.

'Oh, quite reasonable really,' she replied airily. 'I'm glad you're satisfied, Professor Slocombe—and the Academic Board.' Satisfaction guaranteed with the great Professor Mayer, her mind added sardonically, and she stifled a private smile. 'Was there anything else?' she asked, glancing pointedly at her books.

'Ah, yes, there was . . . I wanted to ask how you got on today without Professor Mayer? You and Bill Jones?'

'Fine, thanks. We were rather surprised not to see him, but we didn't . . .'

'You see, I've had a message. He was sorry he couldn't—er—make it. He won't be able to make it tomorrow either, for the tutorial. Do you think you can cope?' He looked at her anxiously.

'Of course I can cope,' she snapped. 'I've always coped, haven't I?' The irritation in her tone was not really aimed at the unfortunate Professor Slocombe, but he wasn't to know that, and cringed visibly.

'Of course you have, my dear; of course. I just thought you should know—after all, he's been there every time so far, and you might have wondered . . .'

Tess felt apologetic. 'I'm sorry, Professor, I didn't mean to sound . . . to be rude.' With an effort she kept her voice steady, even managing a smile. 'Did he say why he wouldn't be able to make it—and why he didn't come today?' She wished her insides would stop churning as if they'd had bad news.

'Well, I only received the message second-hand, from the Secretaries' Office. In fact they took it some hours ago—before your session with Dr Jones—but I've only just got in and picked it up. It seems he is—er—unwell.'

'Unwell?' It was all she could do, now, to keep the harsh concern out of her tone. 'Did he say what was the matter?'

'As I said, Tess, all I have seen is this message.' He took a crumpled scrap of paper from his pocket and read the words on it. ' "Professor Mayer regrets that he is unwell, and will not be able to attend his commitments in

the College today or tomorrow." Not very informative,'
he commented.

'Not very.' She was in control of herself now. 'I hope
it's not serious.'

'Naturally, we all do.' The Professor glanced closely at
her, then looked down at his folded hands. 'If you need
any help or advice while he's away, you will tell me,
won't you, Tess? You're doing—er—manfully, if you'll
pardon the expression, so far—but . . . well, if Professor
Mayer can't be here to add his support to your new
venture . . .'

She smiled warmly at him. Underneath the dry exterior he was a kindly man. And not, perhaps, such a
short-sighted one as all that. 'We'll manage very well,
Bill and I—please don't worry. I'm sure he won't be
away long—I expect he's been attacked by one of our
great British 'flu bugs or something.' She hoped it wasn't
that: if he had been brewing that two nights ago, it would
only be a matter of time before she went down with it
too.

'Professor Mayer does not strike me as the type of
man who goes down with 'flu bugs,' remarked Professor
Slocombe perceptively.

'No.' Tess hoped her colour wasn't rising. 'Well,
anyway, whatever it is, he won't let it keep him away for
too long—from his College commitments,' she said
hastily. 'I know what a lot he has to do.'

'I don't suppose it will. As long as you are prepared
to—er—carry on without him for a day or two. I shall let
you know, of course, as soon as I have news of his
return.'

'Please do that,' said Tess. 'And thanks for telling
me.'

'You have a right to be informed,' he pointed out,
getting up to go. 'And I did want to tell you that

your—er—efforts have not gone unnoted by the Board.'

'Thank you, Professor.' She put her glasses on and bent her head over the books until he had left the room. Then, when the door had clicked behind him, she took them off again and stared vaguely into space for a long time.

So Josh was ill—or something. Was he really ill? Or did he just need an excuse not to come in? Would he, by any chance, be avoiding her? But if he was regretting . . . Monday night, wouldn't he come right out and say so?

It was all probably perfectly straightforward. He was under the weather, and would reappear in a couple of days, the same as ever. Perhaps he would phone her this evening. Yes, he probably would, she decided, and used all her willpower to return to the job in hand.

But he didn't phone that evening, either. Tess stared long and hard at her telephone, willing it to ring; but it remained obstinately silent. A watched phone never rings, she told herself, and set about some energetic housework to keep her mind occupied and her nerves steady. She slept badly, and awoke aching and irritable, wondering how she would get through the General Arts tutorial without him.

She did, of course—and the rest of the day too, somehow. As she walked in through her front door in the evening, her telephone was ringing. Dropping her bags on to the floor, she leaped to answer it, her heart thumping.

'Miss—er—Dr Hope?'

Her heart sank. The voice was male, but there the resemblance ended. 'Yes.'

'It's the Water Board here.'

What, all of it? her mind interjected sarcastically; but all she said was: 'Oh yes. Any news about my river?'

'I'm only calling to tell you we still have the matter in hand. I'm afraid we have no further news for you yet, but we're looking into it.'

'That's kind of you. So you don't know exactly what it is? Whether it's the Fleet, or what?'

'We can't be sure yet, madam,' he explained patiently. 'But we're carrying out our investigations. By process of elimination, it does appear to be the most likely explanation, so far.'

'Oh, good.'

'Good?' He sounded faintly surprised.

'Well, I mean, it's better to know the reason for a thing. Isn't it?' she demanded. She didn't care to tell him how much she wanted it to be the River Fleet—to provide a link with the past, and the present, in such a tangible form. The Water Board, with its head screwed firmly on to its shoulders, would surely find that foolish and fanciful.

'I suppose you could look at it like that, madam,' he was agreeing doubtfully. 'I also wanted to ask, what is it doing now? Is it still the same—any higher or lower?'

'I haven't looked today—you just caught me as I came in. But it was the same yesterday. No different at all. Just . . . flowing gently through the cellar.'

'Fair enough. Important to check up. If it does anything dramatic, you would tell us, wouldn't you, Miss Hope?'

'Don't worry. If it did anything dramatic, you'd hear about it pretty smartly,' she promised vehemently. 'Why, what's it likely to do?' she asked suspiciously.

'Oh, nothing, most likely. But it pays to keep an eye on these things.'

'I'll do that all right. It's my cellar, don't forget,' she pointed out, 'I'm not going to stand by and let myself get flooded out.'

'Okay then. We'll be in touch soon.'

'Thanks for the bulletin,' she said. 'Goodbye.'

She replaced the receiver and sat with her head in her hands, still wearing her coat. Fritz sidled up to see what was the matter. Sitting on the floor in front of her, he gazed enquiringly up through round yellow eyes. A cup of tea often put things right, he suggested, purring—and while he was on the subject, how did she feel about opening a tin for him? He didn't know about her, but he'd had a hard day, and a small snack never came amiss on a chilly afternoon.

Sighing, Tess picked him up and held him close to her. His fur was soft, his little body warm—but she knew his company could never again be a substitute for that human intimacy she had so recently, so powerfully, discovered.

With a final scathing glance over her shoulder at the silent telephone, she set about her evening routine—keeping things going; not letting go. At ten o'clock, when the television programme she was trying to watch merged once and for all into a meaningless jumble in front of her eyes, she switched it off and went into the hall. With a determined set to her mouth she reached for the receiver again.

'Hallo?'

'Hallo, Hil, it's me—Tess.'

'Tess! Are you all right?' They rarely called each other unless there was anything very important to discuss or arrange.

'Yes. No. I don't know.' Her voice trembled. 'I'm not sure, Hil.'

'What is it, love?' Her friend could be very gentle when she wanted to. 'Tell Auntie Hil all about it.'

Tess took a deep breath. 'It's Josh.'

'Ah!' The one word spoke volumes.

'No, you see—he hasn't—I mean, things were going
. . . fine . . .'

'Good.' Hilary tried to sound encouraging but not
too intrigued—a difficult feat which she very nearly
accomplished.

'But then he hasn't been in since Monday, and . . .'

'I thought I hadn't seen him about. Why not?'

'He's ill, apparently.'

'Oh dear! Hasn't he phoned you?'

'No.' Tess paused. 'I only know because Prof
Slocombe told me. He was . . . unwell, the message
said: that's all. I saw him on Monday night and he
seemed okay then.' Okay! That was one word for it, she
supposed. 'It must have come on rather suddenly.'

'You sound sceptical, Tess. Don't you think he really
is ill?'

'I don't know what to think. We got rather . . . carried
away . . .'

'Oh, Tess!' Hilary tried, and failed, to keep the delight
out of her voice.

'Yes, well . . . I expected to see him, or at least hear
from him, after that.'

'Yes, well,' her friend agreed, 'you would. But you
haven't?'

'Not a word—not a squeak. Not a . . . vibe. Nothing.'

'Has he got your phone number?' Hilary wondered
hopefully.

'Of course—I gave it to him when we first . . . He
didn't give me his, but I . . .'

'Why not?' Hilary interrupted, surprised.

'Why didn't he give me his?' Good question, now she
came to think of it. 'He muttered something about it
being unnecessary because we can always see each other
in College to make arrangements, and he was hardly
ever at home anyway, and he couldn't remember it at

that moment and he'd left his diary in his other jacket, and then we changed the subject—you know . . .'

'Hmmm.' The line vibrated with suspicion. 'Sounds strange to me. I mean, I know you said he hadn't told you the address, but I'd have thought . . .'

'So would I,' Tess acknowledged miserably, 'only I just didn't think at all. It's all been so sudden. At first I was deliriously happy, but now I haven't seen him or heard from him all week, and I can't get in touch with him, and he doesn't get in touch with me, and he's supposed to be ill . . . I'm starting to wonder what it was all about.'

'Yes, you would,' Hilary said again. Then she realised she wasn't being as helpful as she might be. 'Look, Tess, maybe he really is ill?'

'Too ill to give me a quick call?'

'I see what you mean,' Hilary admitted.

'He managed to phone College the other day and tell the secretaries.'

'That's an idea. Get them to give you his number—they always have them.'

'I couldn't! They'd never let me have it—they aren't supposed to give away personal information. And anyway . . .' Tess faltered.

'What?' Hilary prompted.

'I don't know if I want to phone him, Hil. I mean, even if I have . . . gone in over my head, fallen the whole way, like you said . . .'

'Did I say that?'

'Words to that effect. Even if I have, I don't have to give up every last shred of dignity and go scraping about for his phone number. He ought to be phoning *me*, Hil.'

'He ought to be. But men don't always do what they *ought* to be doing,' the other woman reminded her in dry tones. 'Sometimes we just have to swallow our pride and take the initiative.'

'It's not taking the initiative I mind,' Tess assured her. 'I wouldn't be very liberated if I did, would I? No, it's just that—as he didn't see fit to give me his number—I can't help suspecting he didn't want me to use it.'

'That's his hard luck. He should have thought of that before leaving you in unexplained silence all this time.'

Tess felt better, as she had known she would, hearing Hilary's commonsense reaction. 'He should, shouldn't he? Thanks, Hil. I'm sorry to drag you into my problems: I feel I'm behaving like a hysterical teenager.'

'Not in the least,' Hilary said firmly. 'Or at any rate,' she added, with a spark of humour, 'no more than you had coming to you after all these years, as I said the other day. Don't worry, Tess, it'll work itself out. Whether you phone him or not . . . something's bound to happen eventually.'

Tess wished she could be so sure. At this moment there didn't seem to be any future in it; nothing but a brief, ecstatic past. She changed the subject. 'How's the family?'

'Oh, fine—I think. I don't seem to see much of them these days. We've promised ourselves a nice quiet Christmas—just the five of us—to catch up.'

'Sounds great,' said Tess enviously.

'You can come if you like,' Hilary invited, with total sincerity.

'Oh no, I won't intrude—but thanks anyway. I expect I'll go to my mother, as usual.' She sighed. It seemed a long time till Christmas, but she supposed it would creep inexorably up on her as it always did. It had never been her favourite time of year—a time for families, and sharing, and warmth . . . 'I mustn't keep you, Hil. I expect I'll see you tomorrow. But I did want to talk to someone tonight.'

'I quite understand,' said Hilary quietly. 'And you never know—he might just turn up at College tomorrow. Then you won't have any difficult decisions to make.'

'He might,' Tess agreed, without much conviction. 'But I have a feeling he won't.'

She was right. Josh did not turn up, nor did he phone. She put off the evil hour of going to the secretaries' office to ask for his number, just in case any message came through. She took her classes, planned her courses and marked her essays as she always did—no less carefully or conscientiously, without a sign of her inner tension. She met Hilary for a very brief word at lunchtime.

Then, just before going home, she took her courage in both hands, squared her shoulders, held her head high and marched down the corridor to the Arts Faculty offices. There she knocked on the door and went in.

The two secretaries were packing up to leave; both of them turned to smile at her. Jane, who organised things for the History and English Departments, knew her well. 'Hi, Tess. What can we do for you?'

'Hallo, Jane.' She forced the most natural smile she could manage, hoping her voice was steadier than it felt. 'I wonder if you can do me a favour?'

'Sure—I mean, I'll try. I'm no fairy godmother,' the pretty blonde girl pointed out, 'but if it's something nice and simple . . .'

'Oh, very simple.' Tess swallowed. 'You know our eminent visitor, Professor Mayer . . .'

The two secretaries exchanged expressive glances. 'I should say we do!' Jane put one hand over her heart, rolling her big blue eyes heavenwards. Sally, the other girl, giggled. Tess looked at them both enquiringly, dark brows raised. 'He's the most gorgeous hunk of male person who's ever set foot in these dowdy old rooms,' Jane explained, with a mock sigh of yearning. 'We both fell in love with him the moment we set eyes on him.'

Sally nodded her agreement. 'Gorgeous,' she echoed, her glasses positively steaming up with enthusiasm.

Tess cleared her throat. 'Yes, well . . . what I wanted to ask . . .'

'Didn't *you*, Dr Hope?' Sally interrupted, reluctant to lose sight of this gripping topic.

'Didn't I what?' Tess forced herself to look puzzled. If they went on like this, she'd get flustered and lose her cool—and then probably give up her brave enquiry altogether.

'Fall in love with him? The moment you set eyes on him?'

'Not exactly.' Not quite straight away, her mind added: it took a few days. 'We work together,' she reminded them crisply.

'Lucky old you!' Jane grinned, then came down off her private fantasy. 'So—what do you want to know? He hasn't been in this week—he's ill. But you must know that already, surely?'

'Yes, I knew that. The thing is, I need to consult him urgently about something. Something to do with the course we're running jointly.'

'I thought Dr Jones was helping you?' Sally wasn't making things any easier.

'Yes, that's right. But this concerns a point which only Professor Mayer and I know about. Something Bill Jones wasn't in on.' Any minute now she was going to blush and give everything away to their keen young eyes. 'I need to know . . . to check a particular reference for next week.'

'He'll probably be back next week,' Jane pointed out. 'He only said he was "unwell"—that could mean anything—but he looks a tough sort of bloke to me. I'm sure he can't be *that* ill.'

'Tough—yes, that's the word,' Sally mused dreamily.

Tess struggled not to show her irritation. 'I need to know *now*,' she said, more sharply than she had intended. 'Can you let me have his phone number at home? I'm sure he's well enough to answer one small question.'

There, it was said. They regarded her speculatively, then they turned to each other. 'What do you think?' Jane asked her colleague.

Sally shrugged. 'Don't see why not. I know we're not supposed to—but they *are* working together, and if Dr Hope needs to ask him something *now* . . .'

They exchanged grins, then Jane turned to Tess. 'We think we'll divulge this piece of personal data—just this once. If,' she went on gravely, 'you promise not to make a habit of it, Dr Hope. It would be more than our jobs were worth if we kept giving people's phone numbers away.'

'Good lord, no. Anyway,' she reminded them, 'I know everyone else's already. We don't usually keep ourselves incommunicado in this Faculty. We try to stay on social terms. For some reason, Joshua Mayer prefers to keep his private life strictly private,' she added tersely.

'So would I, if I looked liked him.' Jane opened a card index and ran a manicured fingernail along the top. 'G . . . H . . . J . . . here we are, M. Mayer.' She drew out the relevant card, putting it down on the desk in front of Tess. 'Copy it for yourself while I finish packing up.'

'Thanks, Jane. You're a friend in need.' Tess tried not to sound too grateful, but her heart was pounding as she got out her pen and diary to copy it down. She glanced at the card: not only the number, but the address as well—an unexpected bonus.

She wrote down the number, and memorised the address. It was easy enough. She knew it well—a quiet square in the very centre of Hampstead Village, lined with stately houses and luxurious mansion blocks— elderly and dignified, rather than new and brash, as befitted that part of London. Hardly a stone's throw from the Heath, and, no doubt, enjoying commanding views across it, and out over the City itself. She had never been inside one of them, but she knew their outsides well enough. She might have guessed it would be somewhere like that.

'Bless you,' she said briskly, putting her pen away and closing her diary on the precious number. 'I'll give him a ring this evening, or tomorrow. He'll quite understand why I needed to, when I explain.'

'Just as long as he isn't angry with us when he finds out how you got hold of his number,' said Jane.

'I'll take full responsibility,' Tess promised. 'I'm sure he won't be.'

Sally was off again. 'A man like that—he could be really wild, if anyone got his blood up.' Her gaze was fixed far away. 'I wouldn't like to be on the wrong side of him, I know that.'

'Wouldn't mind being on the right side, though, eh?' Jane grinned at her suggestively.

Tess retreated hastily. 'Thanks again. Have a good weekend,' she called, leaving them to their girlish prattle. She had had about as much of it as she could take.

When she got home, she stared at the number for a long time. There was still a chance Josh might ring, so she didn't try it at once. She had to plan what she would say—what line she would take. Now that she was confronted with the possibility of talking to him, none of it seemed quite so simple. Perhaps she did mind taking the initiative, after all.

Only four nights ago she had been with him here, in this very room, on that very rug . . . and her life had changed in the space of two hours. It seemed a world away—a universe. And yet, if she let it—if she closed her eyes to allow those recent memories to drift over her— they became the only reality. All the rest of her activities, her preoccupations, her needs, simply faded away to insignificance. Wanting Josh was a dull ache, invading every part of her, every second of every day. Faced with him again, she knew it would be fanned instantly into that fierce flame which had consumed her. She accepted that.

But did he accept it? If so, why had he not rung her? She wanted to know the truth, of course; but was she strong enough to take it? Suppose it was as she feared in her inmost heart: he had been flooded with regret after their close encounter, unable to face her again? Unable to tell her that it had been no more than a momentary aberration, nothing but the fulfilment of a superficial appetite? Unable to tell her—because he knew full well that, for her, it would be a very different story.

She went to sit by the telephone, her mind still churning over the possibilities. She sat there so long that Fritz decided he might as well join her, so he curled up on her lap and went comfortably to sleep. At last Tess pulled herself together; it was no use going round in interminable circles. Action was called for. She opened her diary to read the number again—not that it wasn't engraved on her memory by this time—and picked up the receiver to dial it.

Her finger shook, but she dialled it. With her free

hand, she stroked Fritz for support. He woke up enough to purr appreciatively.

The ringing tone went on for a long time. Josh wasn't going to answer. He was out; he had company. He was too ill to come to the phone, all alone in his flat; he was dead. He had never really existed at all; he had been a figment of her fevered imagination—the frustrated fantasy of a confirmed spinster in need of . . .

The ringing tone was interrupted by a click: someone had answered after all. She gulped, ready with her rehearsed speech: this was it. She waited for him to speak.

'Hallo?' The American voice gave the number she had just dialled. Tess gulped again. It was the wrong voice. It had the right accent, but it was the wrong voice; worse than that, it was the wrong sex. It was, quite clearly, female.

Her mouth was dry, stuck together, useless. The voice was becoming impatient. 'Hallo? Can I help you? Who is this, please?'

Tess made a supreme effort, and found some words. 'Could I . . . is that . . . I wish to speak to Professor Mayer, please.'

'Josh?' There was an edge of hostility, even suspicion, in the voice now. 'Who is this?' it repeated. It sounded positive, Tess thought—confident.

'This is a . . . colleague of his, from the College. I wanted to ask him something.' Well, that was true, as far as it went.

'I see.' Was there relief in the voice now? 'Well, I'm afraid Professor Mayer is sick. He can't come to the phone; he's not allowed to leave his bed.'

Not allowed to leave his bed! As ill as that? Tess's initial shock at encountering a female voice in Josh's flat gave way to genuine fear for his health. Even if he had

. . . deceived her, she had no wish to hear that he was as ill as that. 'I had no idea he was so bad . . . what's wrong?' She couldn't help herself: she had to know.

'He has a fever,' the voice informed her tightly. Obviously a cagey lady, not about to give much away to casual callers; especially female ones.

'A fever?' Tess licked her dry lips. 'But what . . . how . . . ?' She could hardly enquire how it had come up so suddenly, or whether it was infectious. 'I mean—isn't he any better?' she tried lamely.

'Getting a little better every day,' the voice assured her briskly. 'But still not well enough to get up. It's nothing catching,' it went on, as if reading her thoughts. 'His colleagues are perfectly safe, Miss . . .'

Tess did not oblige by supplying the other woman with her name. She had no wish in the world, suddenly, for Josh to know she had asked after him. 'Well, I'm sorry to hear it,' she declared, forcing her tone back to its normal, poised level. 'My question was not that important. Please tell Professor Mayer we all wish him better, and look forward to seeing him when he recovers, Miss . . .'

Josh's companion was more forthcoming than Tess had been. 'The name is Ashley Dean,' she drawled. 'And don't worry,' having presumably convinced herself that Tess was simply an impersonal acquaintance, she could afford to be charitable, 'I'll see he gets over it. He's in good hands.'

'I'm sure he is.' Tess fought to suppress a mounting bitterness. 'Thank you, Miss Dean. Sorry to have troubled you.'

'No trouble. Shall I tell Josh you called?'

'Don't bother him, if he's that ill,' said Tess. 'It'll keep.'

'Okay. 'Bye then.'

'Goodbye.' Tess replaced the receiver in its cradle with a crash. Fritz woke with a start, glaring accusingly at her—she wasn't usually given to making sudden loud noises. She glared back at him. 'The bastard!' she gritted ferociously. 'The unprincipled, unmitigated bastard!'

Fritz had rarely seen her so angry. He couldn't recall having done anything to deserve it recently; but just to be on the safe side, he stretched delicately, then jumped off her lap and stalked down the corridor towards the kitchen—taking his time. A safe distance away, he stopped and sat on the floor, washing one hind leg but keeping a wary yellow eye on her all the while.

'He's the worst kind of a male snake!' Tess ranted. 'The lowest of the low! The absolute dregs! Thank God I found out . . .'

But not in time, her mind taunted cruelly; not before she had made that ultimate commitment, emotional and physical—foolish, naïve young woman that she was. Josh had taken full advantage of her innocence; and she deserved it. Not married, he had said. Oh no, he wasn't married—it had been nothing but the truth. But he had never said he lived alone.

When she thought about it, it all fitted together. Of course he didn't live alone: that was why he was always in a hurry to get back—why he hadn't given her his address or number. He had been two-timing her; but he had been two-timing someone else as well—this . . . whatever her name was—Ashley Dean. His mistress; his girl-friend. His—what was the modern expression that always made her laugh?—LTR: Living Together Relationship. A ridiculous phrase, but so apt. Maybe he'd never had a wife, but he'd had a few of those; he had one now, and she was here in London with him. As she had been all along—all the time he was getting round

Tess, getting what he wanted out of her, at work and at play . . .

She had been a fool; but it was over now. Let him go on being ill as long as he liked; at least she had found out the truth for herself. With any luck, by the time he had got over his mysterious fever, she might have recovered from hers, too.

CHAPTER EIGHT

Down in Brighton, November gales lashed grey seas into heaving rage; and Mrs Marjorie Hope was surprised to receive a telephone call on Saturday morning from her daughter in London.

'Mother?'

'Tess, my dear! Is everything all right with you?' It wasn't long since her last visit: surely not time yet for another dutiful trip to the coast?

'All right, thanks, Mother.' She didn't sound very sure, but it was not Mrs Hope's way to pry into her daughter's affairs—if, that was, she ever had any affairs; if she did, she never confided in her mother about them.

'It's always a pleasure to hear from you, of course, Tess, but is there . . .'

'Yes, there is,' the younger woman cut in with more than usual terseness. 'I need to get out of London. Could I come and spend the weekend at the flat with you? Please?'

'Spend the weekend here? But we haven't got a spare room!' Marjorie Hope's tone was blatantly astounded at such a suggestion.

'I know, Mother. I know you haven't got much space. I'll sleep on the sofa, gladly. On the floor—I don't mind. Just as long as I can spend a night or two away from here. Please, Mother—I wouldn't ask, only I don't know anyone else, and if I could just . . . get a breath of sea air . . .'

Marjorie Hope was not so old, nor so cold, that she failed to recognise a cry for help from her only daughter.

'My dear girl, if it's that important, I'm sure Stella and I can manage something. It's just that you've never wanted to stay before—and when you do come, you're always keen to get off back . . .'

'I know, Mother,' Tess said again. Her voice was carefully controlled but strangely toneless, as if it was an effort keeping it normal. Even down the long-distance wires, Mrs Hope could pick up those tense vibrations. 'I realise it's ridiculously short notice, and it'll be an imposition, but I'll only stay a short time, and I'll bring my sleeping bag, and I'll go out for walks, and I won't eat much . . .'

Her mother laughed outright. 'Tess, you could never be such an imposition as all that! I think we can find the odd morsel to feed our only niece and daughter. It's always a pleasure to see you. It was just that you took me by surprise. Come as soon as you like, and stay as long as you like.'

'Thanks, Mother. I promise not to make a habit of it. I'll catch the first train I can, and probably be with you by lunch time.'

Mrs Hope found the fleeting thought crossing her mind that it might be rather nice if Tess did make a habit of it; but all she said was: 'Very well, dear. We shall look forward to seeing you very soon. And Tess,' she added, just as Tess expected her to ring off in her usual brisk fashion.

'Yes, Mother?'

'I am your mother, after all. You shouldn't be afraid to ask me . . . anything.'

'Yes, Mother. I mean no, Mother.' Tess felt awkward. Her relationship with Marjorie had never been the kind in which one could 'ask anything'. Surely it was too late now, after all these years, to embark on that sort of honesty?

But then again, she reflected as she sat in the train two hours later—perhaps it was never too late to change such deep-rooted habits. Perhaps it was high time she made the effort to get closer to Marjorie. Her mother, who had been a woman of the world—an experienced, cultured woman—well before Tess was even born. Perhaps she had wasted the possibilities of their relationship.

She sighed, gazing out of the dirty window as suburbs gave way to strips of dingy green, and then to less dingy fields, with real cows and sheep in them, and trees, and a real river meandering through them—above ground, untramelled. The countryside! Tess breathed more deeply, even in the stuffy air of the carriage. Her instinct had been right: it was good to get out of the city. A change of scene was absolutely necessary if she was to think over her situation, assess her feelings. Weigh up the profound damage that had been done, against the overwhelming delight she had learned about.

She was fond of Brighton, especially in winter, when the permanent residents were left to enjoy the dignified Regency architecture in peace. At the station the air felt damp and cool. On the front, she knew, it would be bracing; she longed to walk by the sea, allowing her thoughts to run free in the fresh wind. For the moment, she caught a bus which took her to Seven Dials; then she walked the half-mile to the complex of retired people's flats where her mother and aunt lived.

They were waiting for her, quiet and contained as always, with a light lunch of soup, bread and cheese. They took one look at her pale tense face, her shocked, withdrawn eyes, and exchanged wise glances which warned each other to tread cautiously. By mutual unspoken agreement, they treated the younger woman with more gentle kindness than usual—but they didn't probe. When she went out after lunch, pulling on her warm coat and hat, they said nothing; and when she returned some three hours later, flushed but comparatively composed, they offered her tea and scones—and silent sympathy.

She was gratefully aware of their support; and they knew that she was. For the first time in many years Tess, her mother and aunt felt at ease with one another. There was no need to discuss the state of the nation; it was quite obvious that one of them, at least, had far more pressingly private matters on her mind—and the other two respected them even if they had no idea what they were. They had been young once, and their imaginations were far from rusty. It wasn't difficult to guess that whatever Tess's problem was, it had nothing to do with the objective world outside her, and everything to do with her own inner emotional one.

'If she wants to tell us about it,' Marjorie remarked to Stella that night as they made their bedtime drinks in the kitchen—having left Tess snugly ensconced in her sleeping-bag on the sofa—'she'll do so in her own good time.'

'Indeed she will,' agreed her younger sister, secretly hoping that she would, and before too long. She was consumed with curiosity to know what had finally cracked the apparently impervious veneer Tess presented to the world. She had begun to suspect that the girl was cut out to be a single-minded career woman; but perhaps, after all, she was going to go the way her mother had gone, so many long years ago, and would surprise them all by settling down.

'I suppose it's more than likely to be . . . a man?' she conjectured delicately, filling two hot water bottles from the kettle.

'Now why should you jump to any such conclusion?' reproached her sister. 'It might be trouble at work. Or health. Or anxiety about this flood in her house. It might be any number of things.'

'It might,' agreed Stella doubtfully.

'In any case,' Marjorie repeated, 'we shall find out when she sees fit to tell us. Meanwhile, it's our duty to remain supportive, Stella, and not to interfere,' she pointed out sternly.

'Yes, Marjorie,' Stella conceded meekly, as she had always done.

The sofa was not comfortable, but Tess slept heavily, exhausted by emotional turmoil, and by walking against the wind through invigorating sea air—and by the fact that she had slept hardly a wink the previous night. The shock of her cruel discovery had stayed with her throughout the dark hours; and when the first fury had worn off there was just a clawing, agonising emptiness left in its place—too numbing and paralysing even to allow tears.

In the morning, she had known what she had to do: get as far away as possible, as soon as possible. Before she could face up to everyday life again—with Joshua Mayer as part of it—she would have to muster all her resources, close up the huge gap in her defences which her encounter with him had ripped open. Almost without thinking what she was doing, she had picked up the phone and dialled her mother's number.

Now she was glad she had done it. If she had thought too hard, she would have dismissed the idea as pointless. Her mother and aunt—elderly, set in their ways, unforthcoming—were the last people to turn to at times of crisis, weren't they? She should go to Hilary, or . . . or who? There was no one else. She had plenty of acquaintances, but no other real friends—her own careful independence had seen to that. And her mother, when all

was said and done, was still her mother—as she herself
had so unexpectedly reminded her.

Now their undemanding affection was soothing, if not
healing. After another day, or perhaps two, she'd feel
strong enough to return to London and put a brave face
on things. It would be skin-deep, of course; but over the
months she would work on the wound until it began to
close up, until the intense pain became a dull ache, and
scar tissue began to form over the rawness.

On Sunday she took a bus out of the town and walked
across the Downs, an ocean wind pulling her hair in all
directions and clutching greedily at her clothes. She
smiled, exhilarated, as it howled around her—opening
out her arms to welcome it, alone on a grassy clifftop.
Far away below, it was busy churning the surface of that
solid winter sea into a frothing mass—much more exciting, she decided, than its green, glazed summer sheen. It
matched her mood, that was for sure: sombre, seething
and grim.

On Monday morning she made a quick call to the
College. 'I'm not too well,' she told Jane succinctly. 'I'll
be away today and maybe tomorrow as well.'

'I'm sorry to hear that, Tess.' The secretary sounded
genuinely concerned. 'Nothing serious, I hope?'

'Not at all,' Tess stalled, unwilling to invent an
ailment. Born under the sign of Virgo, she was
almost obsessionally honest by nature.

'Bet you've caught something nasty from our great
Professor Mayer,' Jane joked, little suspecting how
painfully close to the truth she came. 'Did you get
through to him on the phone, by the way?' she went on,
relieving Tess of the necessity to reply to her first
facetious comment.

'Yes, thanks. I got through to his flat,' Tess amended
accurately. She kept her voice well under control. 'Is he

back today?' she enquired nonchalantly.

'Not yet—still off sick. We had a phone call just now, as a matter of fact, from a woman, telling me so. A friend of his, perhaps?' Jane suggested archly.

'Perhaps.' Tess's tone and expression were stony.

'Well, anyway,' continued Jane, having failed to achieve a satisfactory impact with this piece of gossip, 'she thought it would be at least another week. He's still not even able to talk on the phone, apparently. Must be something really bad, to go on this long. Poor man,' she sighed sympathetically. 'Mind you,' she added, 'whoever the woman is, I wouldn't mind being in her shoes. Even the job of nursing the lovely Joshua wouldn't come . . .'

'Yes, well, I'm sorry,' Tess interrupted, unable to take any more of the topic. She could picture Sally, in the background, swooning in unison with Jane. 'I must go now. Please tell Professor Slocombe I'll be in as soon as I can, and I'm very sorry to be a nuisance. I hope Dr Jones can cope with our course for a couple of days—he should be all right. Oh, and please ask Hilary Raines to take today's lecture for me. She's done it before—she knows where I keep all my notes. It's on *Sir Gawain and the Green Knight*—I'm pretty sure she's quite well up on that one. Tell her I'll do the same for her any time.'

'I'll tell her, Tess. And don't worry. You do sound a bit under the weather. Take care of yourself—see you when you're feeling better.'

'Thanks, Jane.' Tess rang off, relieved. She disliked having to pretend at all, even when it was justified; but she knew there was no way she could have gone into College yet.

At least, when she did, Josh would not be there. Against her better judgment, she wondered for a moment about this unexplained malady—this 'fever',

Ashley Dean had called it. It must be some fever, to lay him this low. Not that she cared, of course, either way. Nothing about him was any business of hers any more. Except in unavoidable professional contacts, he had ceased to exist for her. That was her decision, reached as she walked through the blustering sea breezes; that was the wise, sensible decision, and she was going to stick by it.

It was a much calmer, more collected Tess who took leave of the two elderly ladies on Tuesday morning and set off for the station. Few words had been spoken between them; but they all sensed that a better understanding had been reached as a result of her visit. Tess gave her mother a hug, as well as the usual brief, dry peck on the cheek. 'Thanks, Mother.'

'What am I supposed to have done?' Marjorie retorted sharply. 'Precious little, as far as I can make out.'

'Just been there,' Tess told her simply. 'It may be little; but it is precious.' She smiled directly at her mother. 'I'll tell you all about it one day, I promise. When I . . . when I can.' A shadow of pain darkened her features.

'My dear child,' declared Marjorie Hope with asperity, 'whether or not you choose to divulge your private affairs is entirely up to you. If my presence is all that's required, I shall be at your disposal any time. You know that.'

'We both will, dear,' endorsed Stella. She gave Tess a kiss. 'Look after yourself now, Tess.' For a moment she gazed into her young relative's face, her own brown eyes shrewd in their wrinkled setting. 'Don't fight too hard,' she said unexpectedly.

Her sister stared at her, surprise struggling with disapproval for the upper hand in her expression at this piece of gratuitously intimate advice. But Tess smiled again, sadly. She recognised it as good advice; but she knew that for her, the fight was only just beginning.

Everything at the house was exactly as she had left it—neat, quiet, orderly—empty. Fritz greeted her with dignified enthusiasm. He never suffered when she went away; Mrs Jacobs, next door but one, always made a point of staying to fuss over him when she came round to feed him, twice a day. Sometimes she even sent her children round to talk to him in the evening, in case he got lonely. Tess had known he was in good hands.

In good hands—where had she recently heard that expression? Ah yes, that was where Josh was, of course—in the good hands of Ashley Dean, who would nurse him lovingly through his illness; and who had made quite sure Tess had got the point when she had told her so . . .

She shook herself physically, to force away such dangerous reflections. Putting down her small suitcase, she bent to pick up the letters from the mat. Mostly the kind of dull manilla envelopes she preferred not to be bothered with: bills, a circular, something from the bank . . dry as bones, all of them.

What was this? One from Thames Water, it seemed: perhaps some news about her river? She went to the kitchen and put the kettle on; then she tore open the envelope and took out the letter. 'Dear Madam,' it began, as formal as ever. 'We are pleased to inform you that our investigations into the flooding in your basement are now completed. We have traced the problem to an overflow in the mains conduit. This was caused by obstruction due to extensive building works currently being carried out in your immediate area . . .' An address was named—the street backing on to Tess's—and she thought she knew the place: an old house which was having a total facelift, being restored from a semi-derelict heap to a fine Edwardian residence within sight of her back windows.

'. . . we have now ascertained,' the letter droned on 'that this obstruction has been removed, and we have every reason to suppose that the high degree of dampness in several adjacent properties, including your own should now subside as a result.' Tess couldn't resist a grin at this description of a minor torrent as a 'high degree of dampness'. She wondered how many other occupants had suffered similar problems. The Water Board was certainly not given to overstatement. 'We are sorry,' it claimed, 'that you have been inconvenienced but since the flooding was not—as we originally suspected—due to natural causes, which would have been extremely difficult to overcome, we are now confident that the water will now abate.' She had to read that sentence through several times before making sense of it. 'Please let us know,' it implored, in conclusion, 'if it has not done so within the next few days.'

The letter was dated Monday. After reading it carefully, Tess went down to inspect the cellar. They were quite right: the floor was practically dry. There was barely more than a trace left of the stream which had so recently flowed through it—a small puddle there, a damp patch here, were all that remained of Tess Hope's own private tributary of the Fleet.

Except, of course, that it never had been that, all along. 'Natural causes', the letter said: meaning the river; the purposeful, powerful force which had been harshly driven underground all those years ago when human expansion had found its existence inconvenient It wasn't until this moment that Tess allowed herself to admit just how badly she had wanted that flood to be the River Fleet. And now she had to face the fact that it had been an illusion—no more than a leak in the mains water supply. She should have been relieved: the Water Board had clearly expected her to be, as a careful householder. But she wasn't; she was overwhelmed with bleak desolation—as if the final blow had been struck.

She sat down, where she was, on the cold stone steps; and at last she wept. At last the tears which had been tightly locked up released themselves—running down her cheeks, unchecked, to the floor, as if they could replace that other flood which had been there until two days ago. She cried out her anguish and disappointment and loneliness for a long time. Then she picked herself up and climbed, slowly, wearily, back to the kitchen, where she sat with her mug of tea, returning Fritz's enquiring gaze through bleary reddened eyes.

'If I'd gone on like that,' she told him, sniffing, 'I'd have ended up sitting in a pool of tears, like Alice in Wonderland. Perhaps,' she meditated, sinking momentarily to the depths of self-pity, 'I should just go out and jump in the nearest proper, overground river. What else is left?'

Fritz suggested that she might remember to leave enough food out for him before taking such drastic action; and she smiled weakly through her tearful mask as she stooped to pick him up. 'It's all right, cat,' she assured him. 'I'll do no such thing. Life has to go on, I suppose.'

She made herself eat a little lunch, although her appetite had all but vanished. Then she sat down to organise some work for the following day. It had never been so difficult to concentrate. Misery was even more impossible to overcome, it seemed, than elation. She was grateful for the diversion when Hilary telephoned at teatime.

'Tess, are you all right?'

'Hil, how lovely of you to ring!'

'Thought you might need to see a friendly voice, if you know what I mean.'

Tess managed a limp chuckle. 'I certainly do. I'm okay—a bit down.'

'What's the matter, Tess? Jane said you weren't well. Is that . . . ?'

'It's a bit hard to explain now, Hil. I had a bad shock, Friday night. I'm not ill, really, just . . . shaken up. I had to get away from London, so I've been to see my mother.'

'A shock?' Suspicion crept in round the edges of Hilary's tone. 'Anything to do with Joshua Mayer?' Her opinion of the man, it seemed, was mixed.

'Why should you think that?' Tess demanded—too quickly.

'I don't know. Just that it was all going so well . . . you were so high . . . I did wonder if you might be heading for—you know—a fall . . .'

'I took a fall, all right,' Tess confirmed grimly. There was no point in beating about the bush. 'I found out he'd been . . . less than straight with me. In fact he's been downright deceitful. He's living with someone, Hil.' Her voice cracked; she couldn't help it, saying the words out loud. 'She's there, at his flat. I got hold of the number from Jane, as you suggested, and phoned, and she answered . . .'

'Oh, Tess!' Hilary sounded stricken. 'Why did I ever suggest it?'

'Don't be ridiculous,' Tess snapped. 'I'd have dis-covered soon enough.'

There was a short pause. 'How can you be sure—I mean, that she was . . . ?'

'His girl-friend? She made it pretty obvious—left me

in no doubt. Her attitude was very protective and possessive. You know.'

'I know,' admitted Hilary gloomily.

'Anyway,' Tess pointed out heavily, 'who else would live at his flat, looking after him, nursing him, answering the phone in a proprietorial sort of way?'

'I suppose there's no other explanation,' Hilary conceded regretfully. 'I'm so sorry, Tess. Men can be such bastards,' she said fiercely.

'He's used me—I know that. But I deserved it, in a way. And I don't . . . regret it, Hil. I've decided,' Tess declared firmly, 'to put the whole thing down to useful experience, and go on from here. I'll be more careful next time, at least. Working with him will be the worst, but once I get things on to an impersonal footing again, I think I'll be able to manage it.'

'You're a brave woman, Tess,' Hilary said admiringly. 'I'll help in any way I can. Stay away as long as you need. We'll all cover for you.'

'Thanks, Hil; but I'm coming back while he's still away—which might be for a while yet, according to Jane. It'll be much better if I'm well into the swing of things by the time he shows up. I'll be okay.' Tess sounded far more positive than she felt; but she had to start as she meant to go on, if she was to see the thing through.

'Would you like me to come round tonight, after supper?' asked Hilary.

'No, no. I'm tired. I'll get an early night, and see you tomorrow.'

'If you're sure? Just phone me—you know, any time you feel low.'

'You're a good friend, Hil.' Tess gulped; she must end this conversation, before she disgraced herself by bursting into tears again. 'Thanks for phoning.'

'Don't be silly,' said Hilary. 'That's what friends are for.'

'Oh, by the way—before you go, you might just like to know—my river isn't one after all.'

'How do you know?'

'The Water Board, in its infinite wisdom, has just informed me that it's been no more than a leaky pipe all the time. Another fantasy shattered!'

'I'd have thought you'd be pleased. I mean, it's one less thing to worry about, isn't it?' Hilary speculated.

'I ought to be,' Tess agreed. 'But I'm not. I'd got sort of attached to having what I thought was the Fleet in my cellar. Still . . .' she braced herself, standing straight, head up, shoulders back—practising the new defiant posture she was going to present to the world, 'it fits, in a way. The loss of a dream; the end of an era.'

That was it, she thought later, as she lay in bed wishing sleep would come. The end of an era. Brief, perhaps; unreal, maybe—but definitely an era. The era of Josh Mayer, and the River Fleet—inextricably linked, in her mind and in her life.

Now, the one had left her house—drained away as if it had never been; in fact, of course, it never had been. And she must banish all trace of the other from her heart, even if she was forced to let him stay at the fringes of her life for a few more months. On the fringes was where he belonged, and where he must stay from now on. It was up to her to make sure he was relegated to his proper place there, before he returned to the College. Otherwise she would have to resign her job; and she had no intention of letting the man ruin that part of her life as well. No intention at all.

CHAPTER NINE

THE next three days were the longest Tess had ever dragged through; but by gritting her teeth and calling up all her reserves, she got through them somehow. It could only get easier, she told herself over and over again. There could be nowhere to go from here but up.

But what would it be like when Josh finally reappeared at the College, ready to pick up where he had left off—with the work, and perhaps with her too? How would she feel, with his constant presence reminding her of the devastating revelations he had been responsible for? With his company, no doubt, in spite of her good intentions, kindling those reactions it had kindled before?

Even in his absence, she caught her body out—yearning for the touch of his, trembling and aching when it recalled his hands upon it, his skin against hers. Her stern warnings to it had no effect whatsoever. Her mind might as well be occupying a different world from her heart, which appeared to have developed a will of its own. She would have to rely on the old adage about time being the great healer; nothing else was going to dull the acute pleasure and pain of those memories.

By Saturday she was desperate. The weekend stretched ahead, endless and empty. She must keep busy—organise herself. Hours spent on her own—that was the great enemy. After breakfast she reached for the telephone to call up an old friend she hadn't seen for some time, to suggest a meeting—perhaps a visit to an art gallery, some lunch together. Before she could pick up the receiver, the phone rang, making her jump. Her nerves were on edge; she must take hold of herself.

'Yes?' she enquired coldly into the mouthpiece.

'Tess?'

Her heart missed a beat, if not several beats. All the emotions of the past week tumbled through her—a confused cascade of raging anger, depression, hollow bitterness, anxiety, leaving her breathless, speechless. The voice was weaker, perhaps—less assured, even— but there was no other voice like it in the world. No other voice that had such an immediate, powerful impact on her senses. A single word, and her defences reeled. She gripped the receiver until her knuckles gleamed white. 'Yes?' she repeated, very quietly.

'It's me—Josh.' As if she needed to be told! There was a silence; even if she had wanted to, she couldn't have spoken. 'Tess? Are you there?' Concern crept into his tone. 'Are you all right?'

'I'm here,' she croaked. Then she cleared her throat and made a determined effort to emanate all the poise she was so far from feeling. 'How are you, Josh? Getting better?' Icy politeness was her best weapon, she real- ised. When she reminded herself of the situation, it wasn't so difficult to achieve it.

'I've been pretty bad,' he admitted. His voice certain- ly sounded strangely thin, lacking in vitality. A spasm of sympathy shot through her; but she fought to overcome it.

'So I understand,' she said coolly. 'Strange, wasn't it—one moment you were bouncing with health and vigour; the next, at death's door,' she observed sarcasti- cally.

'That about sums it up,' he acknowledged. 'This thing always hits me that way. I thought I'd shaken it off, last time, but it was still lurking somewhere. The doctors said it shouldn't happen again—shows how much they know,' he said scornfully.

'This thing?' Tess could not suppress a curiosity to know more.

'It's a form of malaria. I picked it up when I was in the tropics, a few years back—comes at me out of the blue. When I have it, I can't move. I can't even get out of bed—I have this incredible fever which goes on and on. For the last ten days I've hardly known where I was, and when I did, I was too weak to get to the phone. This is the first day I've been allowed up. First thing I had to do was call you.'

What was she supposed to do, cheer? So it was true: he really had had a fever. 'I'm very sorry you've been ill, Josh,' she said carefully. 'I did wonder, when I heard nothing from you for . . .'

'It couldn't have picked a worse moment, could it, Tess?' The voice was still warm, deep, eager, beneath its tiredness. She hardened herself against it. 'If only I could have warned you, or seen you again, just once more, or . . .'

'Or?' she prompted acidly, as his words tailed away, helpless.

'I don't know. Tess, you must have thought I hadn't . . . remembered.'

'Remembered what?' She was blowed if she'd make it any easier for him, however ill he'd been.

'What happened. On the Monday night. I want you to know—the first thing I thought of when I stopped being delirious—and in the gaps in between, when it wasn't so bad—was you. Us. I wanted to phone you straight away, but like I said, I couldn't move. And I wasn't letting someone else do it for me.'

'Someone else? Your personal medic? Your nursing

assistant? Your private health team?' It was no use trying to keep the hurt out of her tone.

'Tess, I've been looked after. There's someone with me here—I wanted to explain about that. That's why I'm calling you now. I should have done it before, but . . .'

'There's no need to explain, Josh. I have already been informed that you are in good hands. Miss Ashley Dean was kind enough to issue a bulletin when I phoned to enquire as to your progress.'

There was a short, stunned pause. When he spoke again, he sounded deeply weary. 'So it *was* you. Ashley said someone phoned from the College, but wouldn't leave a message. I wondered—I thought it might be you, but I knew you didn't have the number.'

'As you know,' she reminded him caustically, 'there are ways round such little difficulties. I didn't need to resort to chatting up the College Librarian. I simply asked the Faculty secretaries—no problem.'

'Oh, Tess!' His voice broke. 'I was a fool not to give it to you in the first place. And not to tell you about Ashley, and . . . Tess, it's not what you're thinking.'

'And how do you know,' she demanded, 'what I'm thinking?'

'It's obvious, isn't it? What would anyone think? Anyway, Tess, I can tell by the way you—you sound. I know you very well, remember? Have you forgotten,' he added, 'just how well?'

His tone had become even lower, threaded through with intimacy. Even disembodied, speaking through a machine, he had the power to make her dissolve—as if he was there in the flesh beside her. This was the test she had been preparing herself to face, all this time. She mustn't fail it now.

'So,' she returned, 'it's obvious what I think, is it? Are you going to deny that I'm right? Can you, Josh?' Could he? Was there just the chance, just the possibility, that she might be wrong after all—that he was speaking the truth? She tried to extinguish the tiny spark of hope which was insisting on igniting itself inside her.

'I am, and I can,' he said firmly. 'But not like this, here and now. I can't talk any more, Tess—not over this damned contraption. I hate the things. I need to see you—I want to see you, Tess. Will you come over? Please?'

The desperate urgency of the plea was transparent, even through the exhaustion. This was the last thing she had expected to deal with. What should she do? Her mind raced. 'I don't see,' she said slowly, playing for time, 'how there can be any explanation of Miss Dean's presence in your flat—or in your life—which would make me any more inclined to want to see you again.'

'Tess!' Her name was a falling, despairing cry which went straight to her heart. 'Can't you understand, woman—I'm begging you to come and see me. To forget what you've been through these last days—I can imagine it only too well—and come, for my sake. The last thing I'll ask you, if you like. A final request.' As she still hesitated, he went on, 'Go back to the time before that—remember what we had going for us. Please, Tess! I was foolish, not telling you all about myself. But I couldn't know I was going to get ill. I couldn't help that. I want to tell you now; I must see you now.'

The last five monosyllables were pronounced very deliberately, on a long, exhaled breath, as if his strength had almost completely deserted him. Tess made up her mind. 'I'll come, if it's that important. When? You mean now?'

'Right now.' It was hardly more than a whisper, but the words were vehement. He had wrung himself out.

Suddenly she was flooded with pity and concern. He

was a sick man. What should she do, if he implored her to go to him, but go to him? 'I'll come.'

His soft reply was filled with relief and gratitude. 'You won't regret it, Tess. You'll understand why I had to see you before I could tell you—and anyway,' she could sense him willing his strength to return, and she added her own will to his, 'I can't wait any longer to see you again. Just let me tell you where I live.'

'I know the address,' she assured him calmly. 'Just rest, Josh. I'll be with you in about forty minutes.'

She glanced outside: it was sleeting. Running upstairs, she put on her heaviest jeans, leg-warmers, two thick sweaters, hat, boots and a padded waterproof anorak. Then she rushed downstairs, winding her long scarf round her neck, and out to the shed where she kept her bicycle. Wheeling it through the house and out of the front door, she closed her mind to the wise warnings which crowded into it—advising her not to go, not to let herself be fooled again—and set off along the slippery, busy, uphill roads to Hampstead Village.

It took her half an hour to reach the Square—peaceful, dignified, just as she had remembered it—and to find the number she had carefully memorised in Jane's office. Breathing heavily, red-cheeked from exertion, she stopped to look up at the building itself—a small, select apartment block, purpose-built some thirty years ago. The view from the top, across London and the Heath, was probably stunning; but from down here it was nothing very exciting.

She left her bike with the friendly porter at the entrance desk, who saw her to the lift and told her which floor Josh's flat was on. 'The Professor,' he called him, making Tess smile. Described like that, he sounded like a dried-up academic; and nothing, as she was the first to know, could be farther from the truth.

The lift was elderly, with manually-operated, clanking iron gates—the kind you could see out of as it travelled. She watched as the numbers lit up to register which floor they were passing: three, four, five . . . Josh lived at the top, as she had obscurely assumed he would.

When she emerged through the heavy doors and finally stood outside his flat, her nerve almost failed her. What was she doing here—where had all her resolve gone? All that steely determination to draw a line under the whole affair, evaporated like so much steam? Shouldn't she just turn round and leave now, before it was too late?

But acute curiosity sharpened her fervent desire to set eyes on him again. She rang the doorbell. She must find out the truth, at least—about Josh, and his illness; about her own feelings; and above all, about Ashley Dean— how she fitted into the complex pattern that seemed to be his life.

She was not prepared, somehow, for him to open the door himself. He stood before her, dominating the hallway of his flat—still big and powerful, but strikingly paler and thinner. The illness had depleted that firm, solid bulk, painting lines of stress round eyes and mouth, leaving him an emaciated version of himself. Only the black hair retained its vigour—unruly, dishevelled, more vital than ever in comparison with his weakened body; and those eyes—such a profound, startling light grey, enhanced in the pallor of his skin. In the efficient central heating, he wore faded jeans and a cotton checked shirt. His feet, she noticed, were bare.

'Tess—you came! Thank you.' He smiled; and that hadn't changed.

Nor had her reaction to it. 'Of course I came,' she replied briskly. 'I said I would.' Suddenly awkward, she stared at her boots.

He stepped back, opening the door wider. 'Come on in,' he invited.

She obeyed, walking past him, still not meeting his eyes. 'Should you be up?' She peeled off her outdoor layers and hung them up on an oak coat-stand, looking round at what appeared to be acres of highly polished, dark wood—enough fine old furniture to fill an antique shop.

'Sure. I don't have to stay in bed all the time. Anyway, I'm alone here at the moment. I couldn't let you in any other way, could I?' he pointed out logically. Walking slowly but steadily, he led her into a spacious lounge, where the fittings and trappings were even more venerably tasteful. 'Not my style, really,' he grinned, seeing her staring at it. 'I prefer something a bit lighter—less austere. But this is how my pal James likes to live, and who am I to question his chosen environment, if he's good enough to let me make use of it?'

'At a price?' Tess suggested, walking over to a high window, where the vista that spread itself away below her fulfilled all the promise of the apartment's exalted position.

'At a price,' Josh agreed sardonically, moving to join her—his own gaze, following hers, resting with satisfaction on that wide sweep of London. 'But well worth it, as I said to you once before.'

Suddenly unable to keep up the cool mask any longer, she swung round to face him. The fact that he would be here alone—that he would have got rid of Ashley Dean, temporarily, in order to conduct this interview with her—had never entered her head. It made things more difficult, somehow—more intense. 'Josh, I had no idea you'd been so ill. It must have been dreadful for you. I'm so sorry,' she blurted out, with disarming sincerity. In an involuntary gesture she held out one hand to him, her expression alive with sympathy—her anger instantly forgotten at the sight of him.

He took the offered hand in both his. They were as large, delicate and warm as she had constantly remembered them; they still sent shivers of recognition through every part of her. Whatever explanation he had to give, she wasn't going to push him out of her consciousness that easily. It had been a vain hope right from the start.

Turning, he led her to an elegantly plush velvet couch, pulling her gently on to it after him. Then he put one long arm across her shoulders, drawing her gently, firmly closer. She didn't resist; she moved willingly towards him—and it was like emerging from the heavy shadows of a dark nightmare, into the brilliance of warm reality.

His eyes fixed on hers, he turned her face up to his with his free hand. The illness had only served to add a strange intensity to everything about him. His impact swept over her now, like a flood tide. She could feel his presence quenching her soul—water to a parched throat. When he kissed her, lightly, tentatively, her whole body trembled violently and she drew away, frightened by the strength of her own emotions.

Josh misinterpreted the slight movement. 'I'm not the man I was—I know that.' He was gruff for a moment, even bitter. 'But I'll get over it fast—I always do. Give me a month and you won't know the difference—that's a promise. Meanwhile . . .' he held her at arms' length, those grey eyes lingering on every detail of her face, 'do I put you off? Am I so much a shadow of my former self?'

'No, Josh,' she denied at once, emphatically, 'you don't. You aren't. Or even if you are, it doesn't matter.' She sucked in a long breath, gathering her forces, making her decision. Suddenly it was much easier. 'I loved you then, and I love you now. I've tried to tell myself I don't, but it's no use. I don't care about Ashley Dean, or your malaria, or anything else. I don't blame you for . . . what happened between us. It happened because I wanted it to, and I'll always believe you wanted it to as well.' She flung back her head to gaze straight into his eyes, defiant in her outpouring of honesty. It was a relief, a cleansing, to tell him the truth—and to tell herself, too, after hiding from it so long, so stupidly. 'Even if I never see you again after this,' she declared, 'I want you to know . . . to know that.'

His expression softened; his eyes were indescribably tender as they returned her steady gaze. In a gesture she recalled with a pang, he laid one long finger against her lips. Then he took her in his arms—still strong, still forceful even in their depleted state—and held her very close for a long time.

His words, when he finally spoke, rumbled through her body as if they came from far inside it. His voice was choked, but deep—soft but low. She felt, rather than heard, what it was telling her. 'I'll never forget you saying that to me, Tess. I've missed you so much. Every moment I've been conscious, I longed for you—and even when I wasn't, you were there, somewhere inside my head. When you find out more about me, you might take back what you just said. But I'll never forget that you said it.'

When eventually he released her, he kept her hand tightly in his, as if he was afraid she would walk away. 'Would you like a coffee or something?' he asked, after a short silence. 'I'm not being much of a host, am I?' he grinned ruefully. 'Just being upright is something of a new experience, as yet.'

Tess shook her head, bemused by his change of mood. Whatever he had to tell her, she wished he'd get on and do it. 'No, thanks—I'm fine, really.'

'How did you get over here so fast anyway?' he enquired.

'I cycled.'

'Of course—the pollution-free machine. I've never seen you on it yet—that's a pleasure I have in store. It certainly gives you a most attractive colour.' He lifted a hand to touch her cheek with his warm palm.

She blushed, deepening the already glowing pink there—in such stark contrast to the whiteness of his. 'It's the only exercise I get. And it's cold out today.' Not to mention, she added mentally, the disturbing effect of his proximity upon her senses.

'Thank you for coming, Tess, when I called you. You must have been so . . . hurt.'

'I was, when you didn't get in touch. Then when I found out about Ashley . . .

'But you haven't found out about Ashley,' he interrupted tersely. 'Not yet. Only that she exists. Aren't you still mad at me? Don't you want to know why she's here?'

Tess considered very carefully for a full minute, then she said slowly: 'Maybe the less I ever know, the better. I'm not angry any more, Josh. My instinct tells me you were honest in how you treated me, and that's enough for me. You had your reasons for . . . not telling me everything. Why don't I just go now, and leave it like this—leave you to get better, pretend nothing ever happened between us . . .'

He laid both hands on her shoulders, and very gently, he shook her. 'That,' he retorted, 'is the craziest suggestion I ever heard in my life, Dr Hope!' She tingled with sharp pleasure, hearing the indomitable echo of his spirit returning. 'You pedal all the way over here, at the drop of a phone, just to see me again—looking like a . . . a war victim,' he growled, with that touch of bitterness. 'And then, when you've told me the one thing which is guaranteed to speed my recovery, you want to go away again and leave it right there? Never even hear what you came to hear in the first place?'

She stared down at the glowing parquet floor, dotted with rich Middle-Eastern rugs. 'Put like that . . .' she murmured, confused.

'Put like that, it's the most incoherent, irrational piece of nonsense I've been privileged to hear. Not worthy of the super-controlled, intellectual Mediaeval Studies expert I'd come to know.' Warmth permeated his tone as he added: 'but much worthier of that wonderful lady I'd only just been introduced to, when this confounded bug hit me. That other Tess—the impulsive, generous one, who discovered her own nature and her needs, and reached out and welcomed them . . .'

His voice cracked as he moved towards her, taking her face between his two hands. There was no preventing it this time: bodily weakness, sensible words were forgotten as his mouth claimed hers with the full force and potency of a fit man—arousing responses in her that were firmly in the present, and no mere mementoes of an earlier passion.

As the kiss deepened into fierce demand, his hands left her face to slide down her neck and shoulders, and then to her waist, finding their skilled way under two layers of woollen sweater until the sensitive fingers touched her bare skin; stroking her back, exploring her breasts, bringing them to throbbing life—until the world fell away, became lost in that total sensation of him which she had dreamed about, and tried not to dream about, for so long.

Her own hands clung to him, moulding the shape of his body, registering its muscular firmness even in its wasted state. Suddenly nothing mattered but his close presence, and that overwhelming mutual need which no illness, nor suspicion, nor jealousy, nor anger, could obliterate. She was well beyond understanding herself, let alone Josh. Whatever it was he had to tell her, let it wait; this was a more important—the only important— form of communication.

'Tess!' It was partly a groan, partly a sigh. 'You can drive me mad for you, even now, when I'm like this. What's it going to be like when I'm back to normal again?'

She pushed him away, the words bringing her to her senses. 'Josh, I should never have let this happen. You're ill—it'll be bad for you.' Her voice was husky but emphatic.

'It's the best tonic a man could ask for.' He buried his head between her breasts: she could feel his breath, warm upon her skin, as he murmured against them. 'If I'd had you to nurse me, I'd have got better all the quicker. If I'd seen you every day—a reminder of what I had to get better for . . .'

'I wish I'd been here to nurse you,' she said simply. 'But you were well looked after, weren't you, Josh?' She asked the question directly, without rancour. 'Ashley— she did . . . she knew what to do . . . ?' It wasn't easy, getting the words out. After all, she was talking about her rival—the other woman in his life—his mistress. But somehow, at this moment, all that seemed to matter was Josh—his wellbeing, his recovery.

When he looked at her, his face was creased with tenderness. 'What a remarkable lady you are! It takes quite a person to care more about . . .' He pulled himself up so that he was beside her again; then, drawing her head on to his shoulder, he went on, 'it's high time I told you a thing or two about me. This has gone on long enough. Before we go an inch further, you're going to hear this.'

Tess prepared herself—with trepidation, with resignation, almost—to listen. If knowing the truth was inevitable, she would accept it.

'I don't live alone,' he began.

'I know that.'

'Kindly do not interrupt, Dr Hope,' he reprimanded. 'This will not be easy for me, so kindly refrain from putting your oar in. Okay? When I've finished, you can say what you like—as I have no doubt you will,' he added grimly.

'Okay,' she agreed meekly. 'Sorry, Josh.'

'So I should think. Now, where was I? Ah yes; I do not live alone, Tess. And this wretched little germ isn't the only thing I picked up when I was in the tropics. Five years ago, when I spent a year in Bangkok, I met a girl . . .'

'Ashley Dean?' Tess was unable to prevent the words forming themselves.

He regarded her sternly. 'I won't tell you again: keep quiet, or I'll . . . I'll change my mind about telling you at all,' he threatened.

'Sorry again.'

'She was a Thai. She was a . . . prostitute. Her name was Suree.' He paused, allowing Tess to take this in. Wondering where it was leading, she simply nodded. Nothing about him could surprise her any more. 'I was not a client of hers, as it happens,' he went on. 'I met her when she was attacked in the street one night. I was passing, on my way home. I rescued her from three louts who were about to do something quite unspeakable . . .' he shuddered. 'That's a violent, amoral city, if I've ever been in one. Anyway, I took her to my apartment. She was cut up, bruised and terrified—but otherwise in one piece. I took care of her, till she recovered. We became . . . friends.'

'Lovers?' Tess suggested quietly. This story was far too exotic, too extraordinary to have anything to do with her. That made it easier to take in.

'No, that's not what I said, Tess. Friends. She looked after me—I suppose she became a sort of housekeeper. I looked after her. It was a mutually convenient arrangement.'

'Did you . . . love her?' Tess asked gently, lifting her head to gaze up into his animated face.

'In a way, yes. She was a wonderful girl, all lightness and delicacy—ethereal, not real, somehow. And yet warm and caring too. I became very fond of her, yes— but I wasn't in love with her, no.' With a sidelong glance, he added, 'I prefer my women a bit more . . . substantial.' Tess grinned, wrinkling up her nose at him. 'And I never slept with her, either—though she would have been more than willing.'

I'll bet, thought Tess, becoming more intrigued every minute. 'So?' she prompted impatiently, as he paused to rest.

'So.' Josh took a long breath, gathering his strength. 'She was with me for seven months. Then . . .'

There was a distinct sound of the jangling of keys; a lock turning. The front door slammed; footsteps approached through the hall. They were no longer alone. Ashley Dean had returned. 'Josh!' she called, from outside the room, and Tess stiffened. The voice she had heard on the telephone was unmistakable.

'Damn!' cursed Josh, his face darkening. 'I should have got on with it sooner—I knew they'd be back soon.' He ran an agitated hand through his hair. 'I might have known your presence would distract me from the job in hand, Tess.'

They? What was he talking about? Before she had
time to ponder, the lounge door was flung open, to admit
a slight young woman with a pleasant, bland face, short
neat fair hair, and blue eyes. She wore a pair of old
denims and a sloppy sweatshirt, canvas sneakers and no
make-up. 'Hi!' she greeted them, with an engaging,
youthful smile. 'You must be Tess.'

Her attitude was not what Tess would have expected
from a woman arriving home to discover a female
intruder in her rightful place. And how did she know
who *she* was—it was almost as if she had known Tess was
there? It was all very bewildering.

'Has he been behaving himself?' The American girl
continued, as if she had known Tess all her life. 'He
should still be in bed, but it takes more discipline than I
can wield to keep him there, now he's on the mend.' She
shook her head at Josh. 'You're a wicked patient,
Professor. Only when he was flat out with fever could I
do anything with him at all,' she told Tess. 'And even
then we had to have a nurse in as well.'

Tess glanced at Josh for inspiration; but he wasn't
looking at either of them. His eyes were on the open
door behind Ashley. Then he looked enquiringly at the
girl, who smiled. 'No, I haven't lost him. He's in the
bathroom. He'll be along in a moment.' Now thoroughly
mystified, Tess looked from one to the other, her expression pleading for enlightenment. Ashley's face registered sudden comprehension. 'Josh—you haven't told
her yet! I'm sorry—I really couldn't keep him out any
longer in this . . . it's freezing out there; and wet . . .'

The patter of small feet in the hall strengthened a
suspicion that was dawning in Tess's astonished mind.
Josh continued to stare at the doorway, making no
attempt to speak. He looked resigned, almost glazed—
as if he had given up some kind of inner struggle.

The small footsteps were accompanied by a high voice. 'Josh! Where are you?' It came nearer. It had a musical tone and an American accent. 'Why aren't you in bed? We've been to the . . .'

Its owner arrived in the doorway and stopped short, confronted with a new face next to Josh's on the couch. The voice belonged to a child, of course: a small boy, about four years old. He was very beautiful, and very bright; and everything about him—the smooth round face, the sallow skin, the flat nose, the dark almond eyes, the straight black glossy hair—shouted proudly of his Asian origins.

'This is what I was trying to tell you,' Josh said softly. 'This is Danny,' he explained, as if that made everything clear. 'He lives with me.'

CHAPTER TEN

For a long moment, two pairs of intelligent brown eyes considered each other across the room. Then the boy ran to Josh, who opened his arms to him, lifting the small form on to his lap. From that secure haven, Danny resumed his scrutiny of the visitor.

Tess smiled at him. 'Hallo, Danny,' she said.

Josh hugged the child, smiling at Tess over his head. 'This is Tess,' he told him gently. 'Are you going to say hi to her?'

'Hi,' offered Danny obediently. Then he turned and snuggled into Josh's chest, nestling into the warmth of him, one dark eye peeping out to see if Tess was watching.

She was. The sight of them together—big man and small boy, their mutual affection clear and tangible—brought unaccountable tears into her eyes. She laughed, to hide her emotional reaction, and her amazement, as best she could. 'So,' she addressed Danny lightly, 'you live here too?'

He nodded. 'He sure does,' said Josh, returning her smile while his eyes gazed, pleaded, deep into hers.

From behind them, Ashley spoke, making Tess jump. She had quite forgotten the other woman was there. 'Well, folks,' she said briskly, 'I guess I'll go and make all of us a cup of coffee. Danny, how's about some milk and a cookie? Coming to help me get them ready? You can switch the percolator on.'

'Good idea. Thanks, Ashley,' Josh said gratefully. Danny scrambled off Josh's knee, still glancing shyly in

176

Tess's direction. Then he skipped out of the room behind Ashley, who took his hand as they crossed the hallway to the kitchen.

Tess and Josh were left alone, to stare at each other. It was Josh who broke the silence. 'Well?' he observed.

'Well?' echoed Tess, at a loss for words.

'That's my dark secret. That little person is responsible, single-handed, for keeping me away from you at nights, bringing me home early from wonderful evenings, preventing me from seeing you some weekends . . . just him. No one else.'

'Ashley?' Tess managed to mutter, licking her dry lips.

'Ashley was once a student of mine, about two years ago, till she flunked out of college—failed all her exams.' He grinned. 'She was never cut out for the academic life; but she was great with kids—had four young sisters and brothers. She used to babysit for Danny a lot. Then, when the woman who lived in—my permanent help— had to leave, Ashley stepped into the breach. She's been with us ever since. I had to have someone with me when I came over here. I never leave Danny behind, you see, Tess. I take him with me everywhere.'

'And that's all? She just . . . looks after Danny while you're . . . ?'

'That's about it. The long and short of it. She's a sweet girl, excellent with him. He trusts her; I trust her. But I always like to be there when he wakes in the morning— and at his bedtime too, if I can. And I prefer to be back in the evenings, not too late, because he often wakes up around eleven and asks for me.' He smiled to himself. 'I guess I'm just a soft old dad, when it comes to young Dan. He means a lot to me.' He took her hand. 'And so do you, lady. Maybe you can imagine the kind of conflicts I had to sort out, after I met you?'

Tess was still stunned. 'But, Josh, why didn't you tell me? It changes everything—sheds a whole new light on you. It makes so much sense, now that I . . . Why didn't you tell me?' she repeated, with added, urgent vehemence.

He shrugged. 'You just answered your own question, Tess. *It changes everything. Sheds a whole new light on me*. Why should I want to change anything? It was all going fine. Why should I risk losing you, telling you I was encumbered with a child?'

'*Losing* me?' She could hardly believe her ears. 'But, Josh, he's . . . he's lovely! You wouldn't have lost me, if you'd told me. I'm not that shallow,' she pointed out tautly.

'Not shallow, Tess; but I have found that his existence puts some people right off—the added responsibility, the competition, the inconvenience . . . I don't know.' He released her hand to spread his fingers out, staring down at them. 'Maybe they don't like to see me that way—the devoted father. Maybe it spoils their image of me,' he mused cynically.

'By "people", I take it you mean women?'

'By and large, yes. Women. Potential girl-friends.'

'Like me?'

'None of them was ever in the least bit like you, Tess.' He took her hand again. 'I was all set to tell you about Danny. After that evening—that Monday, which I shall never forget, as long as I live . . .' the glance he shot at her caused her insides to curl up alarmingly, 'I made up my mind that I would, the next time I saw you. And then I had to go down with this damned fever of mine.' He frowned heavily, the beetling brows meeting over the hooked nose in a way that had become as familiar to Tess as her own face in the mirror. 'Believe me, Tess, if you'd asked me my own name during those delirious days, I would hardly have been able to tell you.'

She squeezed his hand. 'It's all right, Josh. I understand everything now a lot of things I didn't understand before. And Danny?' she went on quietly. 'He's something to do with—with Suree?'

He raised one wry eyebrow. 'You could say so. He's her son. She was already pregnant when I met her, but she didn't know it yet then. Seven months later—as I was on the point of telling you just now—he was born; and she died.' Pain filled his eyes as he made the bald statement.

Tess held his hands tightly in both of hers. 'Oh, Josh,' she whispered, 'I'm so sorry!'

'So was I. She was a tiny slip of a girl—built like a kid. He was a big baby. They did what they could, but things were a bit . . . primitive, even though I had the best care I could get. She was very weak, by the time they got round to realising she needed a Caesarian. It was too late, and she haemorrhaged. She was always undernourished; she ate like a bird, even during her months with me. Her early life had been nothing but sordid deprivation and misery—not that she talked about it much and in the end it caught up with her. She was never strong.'

'Poor girl!' Tess was silent, contemplating the sad, alien little life. 'And poor Danny,' she went on, after a moment. 'Who was his father?'

'I don't suppose even his mother knew that for sure,' he replied tersely. 'Could have been one of a large number, I dare say. But he's almost certainly a Thai, through and through. Possibly the father might have been Chinese. But you can see, can't you, Tess, that I had no choice?' He turned to her, his eyes beseeching again. 'I took the baby on, for his mother's sake, and reared him as my own. As far as Dan and I—and the rest of the world—are concerned, he *is* my own. I've legally adopted him. He's my son, as much a part of me as . . . as my own body.'

Tess smiled. 'I can see that. He adores you too. He's sweet, Josh.'

'Don't you mind, Tess?' Anxiety filled his eyes now as they stared into hers.

'Why should I mind? You seem to have this notion that I'm going to turn and flee from your life just because I find there's a child in it too. I think it's wonderful, Josh—and moving. It . . . enriches you. I love you all the more for it. I only wish you'd told me long ago—it must have been hell for you, keeping such a major part of yourself locked away from me.'

'It was,' he admitted simply. 'The more important you became to me, the worse I felt. It was as if the two of you were tearing me apart—and you never even knew about each other.'

'I still can't think why you didn't introduce us,' she persisted stubbornly. 'Think of the trouble it would have saved!'

'I've already tried to explain—I thought it would frighten you off. Don't you remember, Tess, that first time I barged into your house—what you said?'

'I remember several things I said.' The occasion was indelibly stamped upon her memory—but any words which might have been relevant to Danny's existence . . . She frowned, trying to recall some.

'"Children,"' quoted Josh, as if reciting a carefully-memorised part, '"are the last thing my life needs."' Now do you remember?'

She caught her breath. 'But that was . . . that was in relation to Fritz. You accused him of being a "surrogate child", if I'm not mistaken. I had no idea it would mean anything personal to you—how could I, Josh? I didn't connect you with . . . with children.'

'People don't,' he acknowledged drily.

'I thought you were just teasing me for my . . . feminist poses; getting at me for my exaggerated independence. Suggesting I couldn't have a pet without it being any more than a child-substitute. Or even,' she added thoughtfully, 'a man-substitute. That made me furious.'

'Maybe because there was a grain of truth in it?' he risked, with a gleam—ready to back off when she attacked him.

But she merely smiled and raised her eyebrows at him. 'Could be,' she conceded. 'I seem to have shifted my ground a bit since then. Not all the way, mind you,' she added firmly. 'But quite a bit.'

'And I respect you all the more for it,' he assured her warmly. 'So it seems I should have told you about Danny—and Ashley—right from the start. But I thought I was doing the best thing, leaving it. And I never like to let my work colleagues know about him—it seems private, somehow.'

'They'd certainly find it hard to take in, you as a father,' she agreed, smiling to imagine Jane and Sally's reaction to such a piece of news—or Hilary's, for that matter.

'My sisters think I'm crazy,' Josh went on, 'taking him around with me everywhere. They've both offered to have him—raise him with their own. But I won't be parted from him, Tess. He belongs with me.'

'What happens when he goes to school?' she wondered practically.

'A good question—and one that becomes more pertinent every year. You remember all that talk we had about me settling down in one place? Putting out roots?'

'Of course. You must have had it on your mind then.

Didn't Danny's existence make you want to do that at last?'

'Not really. As long as he was with me, I was content to travel around as I've always done. When he was a baby, a Thai woman helped me out till I left Bangkok. Then there was another girl—a friend of Ruth's—for the next two years, while I was in various parts of the States. After that, an elderly woman came, while I was back in Princeton. She had to leave, to look after her grand-children when her daughter got ill. Then there was Ashley, and she's been great. Helping me through this illness was never part of her contract, but she's done it without a murmur. She's pure gold. But now she wants to leave, as soon as we get back to the States next spring, and take a course in nursery nursing.' He pulled a wry face. 'It's my own fault—I guess I've given her a taste for it.'

'You can't blame her for wanting to live her own life,' Tess pointed out gently.

'I don't—no way. But it makes me feel deeply aware of the irregular life Danny's been leading. It didn't seem to matter so much when he was tiny, as long as he always had me, and we both trusted the people who came to help me out. But now he's getting older, he feels it more.' He frowned. 'He needs a more stable home life.'

'So—what will you do?'

'What I've always done—cross that bridge when I reach it. Get through these few months and then see what life throws into my path. Never a dull moment,' he added, pulling her towards him. 'It threw you at me, after all, didn't it?'

Before he could kiss her, there was the sound of voices in the hall. They broke apart. Ashley had taken as long as she discreetly could over preparing the coffee—and

Tess had to admit she was more than ready for a cup after the shocks of the last two hours. Danny trotted through the door, an advance herald, carefully clutching a large glass of milk in his small hands. Ashley appeared behind him, carrying a tray.

'Okay if we two come in?' she enquired.

'Of course.' Smiling, Tess got up to take the tray from her and set it on the glass-topped coffee table.

'Have you folks sorted yourselves out now?' Ashley demanded with endearing frankness. To Tess she added: 'He's been like a cat on hot bricks ever since he was better enough to know what was going on. He couldn't think about anything except phoning you, but he wasn't well enough even to do that. He wouldn't let me do it for him—he wanted to tell you everything himself.' Her blue eyes rested on Josh. 'I'm not at all sure he's up to all this excitement now, really.'

It was true: Josh suddenly looked drawn and grey with exhaustion. Tess was filled with remorse. 'You must get straight back to bed,' she instructed him firmly. 'I'll drink my coffee with Ashley and Danny. You take yours to bed. I'll come and say goodbye to you before I go—I can see you've had all you can take for one day. Go on,' she insisted, as he sat staring at her in surprised, weary amusement, 'do as you're told!'

'Yes, ma'am.' With some difficulty, he got to his feet and made his way slowly across the room. At the door he turned, eyebrows raised satirically. 'Promise you'll come and tuck me in when I'm in bed?' he demanded—present company making it impossible for him to suggest anything more intimate than that.

'I promise. Now get out,' Tess ordered brusquely. He went.

Danny was taking all this in with profound interest. 'I think my daddy likes you,' he announced solemnly after

Josh had made a dignified exit. 'He doesn't always do what people tell him.'

'And what about you?' Tess smiled at the little boy. 'Do you always do what they tell you?'

He contemplated this difficult question. 'If I like them,' he decided.

'And if you don't?'

He took a swig of his milk, which left a white moustache above his upper lip. Then he studied her over the top of the glass, and his face was split by a broad, contagious grin. 'If I don't,' he declared, 'I just don't listen to them.'

Ashley and Tess exchanged quick smiles over their cups. 'That's not true, and you know it,' said Ashley. 'You're a very good boy. You nearly always do what people tell you—as long as they tell you nicely.'

'That,' he pointed out roundly, 'is because I nearly always like them.'

The logic of this was so perfect that both girls burst out laughing. He might not be a son of Josh's by blood, Tess thought; but in spirit he most certainly was.

Two weeks later, on a clear sharp December Sunday, three figures strolled on Hampstead Heath as the sun made its early descent over the western horizon, casting long thin shadows across the close-cropped grass. To be more precise, two figures strolled, hand in hand, while a third—much smaller—ran backwards and forwards and around them in circles, displaying the boundless energy of the very young.

'Can we go to your house today, Tess?' he pestered, for the fourth time in twenty minutes. 'I want to see Fritz.'

'We got the message,' Josh told him. 'You want to see Fritz—okay.'

'But can we?' persisted Danny, undaunted.

'Of course,' she said. 'I was expecting you to. I've got crumpets, and jam.'

'Crumpets? What are those? What's jam? Is it nice?'

Tess was stopped in her tracks by this display of ignorance. 'You've never had crumpets? Or jam? Two of our greatest British institutions?' She glared at Josh. 'Your father is failing to educate you properly.'

'Jam,' he told Danny, 'is what you call jelly.'

'Then what do you call jelly?' Tess enquired, puzzled.

'Jello,' he informed her solemnly.

'Oh good, I like jelly,' Danny said happily. 'And what are those other things you said? Crumbles?'

'Crumpets are a bit like muffins. What we call English muffins,' said Josh.

'They're not a bit like what *we* call muffins,' protested Tess. 'Muffins haven't got holes in for the butter to soak through. Crumpets have.'

'I can see there's a serious language barrier to be broken down in these transatlantic alliances,' observed Josh. 'Good thing,' he added, with a dry glint at Tess, 'that there are other ways of communicating, or we might fail to understand each other altogether.'

'I don't think there's much danger of that,' she countered, returning his grin.

'*You say "tomarto" and I say "tomayto"*,' Josh sang, as they walked on down the hill.

At the bottom, they paused to gaze out over Highgate Ponds. Danny crouched down to talk to a gaggle of ducks who had swum hopefully up to greet them. Josh held Tess's hand more tightly, knowing they were both thinking about the River Fleet. With a lump in her throat, she felt herself, all at once, part of a ready-made family. To think, three weeks ago she had expected never to be close to Josh again—and she hadn't even known this child existed! And now the two of them were her pivot, her reality. It seemed scarcely possible.

'What a pity,' she said to him now, 'I can't think of this water flowing all the way to my house, after all.'

'I don't know. Maybe it was just as well really,' Josh replied thoughtfully.

'Why?' she demanded suspiciously.

'It doesn't look too good when you want to sell a house, if there's a river running through the basement,' he pointed out. 'Now, a stream at the bottom of your garden, perhaps . . .'

'But who says I want to sell my house? It's a very good house.'

Danny appeared at her other side, grabbing her hand, skipping up and down. 'I like your house. It's got Fritz in it.'

Josh smiled fondly at the boy. 'You're kind of keen on Fritz, aren't you?'

'Sure I am. He chases things, and he smiles at me. Can we go see him?'

They laughed—defeated, as usual, by the child's enthusiasm. 'Come on, then, back to the car. I'm getting tired, anyway,' said Josh.

Tess glanced at him anxiously. 'You mustn't overdo it, Josh. You've been getting on so well. Don't spoil it.'

'Don't worry, I won't. Not while I've got you to nag at me, as well as Ashley and Danny. I'm outnumbered,' he told her wistfully.

Later they sat in Tess's warm sitting-room over tea and crumpets, while it grew dark and frosty outside the curtains. Danny and Fritz curled up in the biggest armchair, and both of them fell into a contented doze.

Josh looked over at him sadly. 'He loves animals, but he's never been able to have any of his own because of all the travelling we do.'

'He can come and play with Fritz whenever he likes.'
Tess got up from her chair, licking the butter off her
fingers, and came to sit next to Josh on the rug—that
same rug where they had lain together on another,
auspicious night—it seemed a long time ago, so much
longer than it was. And where, for that matter, they had
lain together on more than one occasion since.

'But we won't be here for ever,' Josh reminded her
quietly. Tess winced; that was something she tried hard
not to think about. The present was too good to be upset
by the future.

'You've still got . . . months,' she said quickly.

'Four, maybe, five at the most. I never was staying the
full academic year. Tess . . .'

'Yes, Josh?'

'What I said about selling your house . . .'

'Yes?'

'Would you leave it? Would you leave London, if
there was a good reason?'

'What sort of reason?' she asked cautiously, though
she understood him well enough.

'Like moving to America with me?'

She sat perfectly still, thinking about it; but they both
knew there was only one answer. 'I'd come with you,
Josh. I'd come with you anywhere—you know that. I
won't pretend I wouldn't rather stay in one place, wherever it was, perhaps get a job. But I could leave the
College any time and never look back. London, too,
even England. I'm not that attached to places; but I'd
miss—you know—working. Having my own thing to
do.'

'Of course you would. How about helping me with my
research projects—would that count as working?' He
gathered her into his arms, nuzzling her dark curls.
Danny shifted in his sleep and snored gently, and Fritz

emitted a loud purr. 'We work so well together, Tess,' he muttered, into her hair. 'In every way.'

'I'd like that a lot, Josh.' She nestled closer to him. 'But I think I might need a project of my own, too. Unless, of course . . .' the glance she gave him now held a new, coy quality.

'Unless what, Doc Hope?'

'Unless a brother or sister for Danny happened to come along. Then I might be forced to reconsider my position, as Bill Jones might say, vis-à-vis other commitments,' she announced with mock pomposity.

Josh laughed then, deep in his throat, holding her even more tightly. 'Tess, I love you. Not only am I in love with you, but I love you too. That's a rare combination—a first, for me. I think I've loved you right from that day in the canteen when you were so righteously indignant, so splendidly outraged, at my very existence.' He hung his head. 'I've made you angry a time or two since then. Even angrier, I'm afraid.'

'It's all water under the house now,' Tess said gravely—and giggled.

'Funny lady, huh?' He pulled one of her tousled curls. 'Even your awful jokes seem to have become indispensable to me, Tess.' Suddenly serious, he moved away far enough to look down into her face. 'Marry me, Dr Hope? Please? Brighten up a poor old History Professor's dreary days?'

She gazed back at him, loving every inch of him; but she didn't answer at once. 'You can keep your own name,' he went on, urgently persuasive now. 'As my partner, or my assistant, or as a lecturer in your own right—whatever you do—but marry me, Tess. I want you for my wife; Danny wants you for his mother. Will you take us both on?'

'Yes, Josh, I will. And names don't mean a thing to

me. Real independence is something deeper than that. I think,' she told him softly, seriously, 'I'm learning that you can't have it, really, without dependence—inter-dependence.' She paused as they both deliberated this profound piece of philosophy. 'But, Josh, there is one thing . . .'

'Anything,' he interrupted eagerly. 'What's mine is yours, you know that.'

'Nothing like that.' She smiled. 'Let's settle some-where, so that Danny can go to school like other chil-dren. I don't really mind where, but let's put down some roots together—make a proper home for ourselves, and him.'

'That's exactly what I intend to do.' Josh took her in his arms again—those strong arms, so nearly back to their old vigour again. 'And I've got one more thing to ask you.'

'Questions, questions!' she complained, into his shoulder.

'Just one more. Come and spend Christmas with my family in the States. Meet them all—see my home, and the University—see the whole place where I grew up. If you like it,' he said, his face as excited as a child's, 'we can go back there and live, next year.'

'Live in Princeton?'

'Why not? I have a feeling the Department there will be only too pleased to have me around on a more permanent basis, after all my gadding about. As for me, I've had enough of all that to last a lifetime. Maybe I need to keep still.' He stroked her cheek. 'Raise a family. What do you say?'

After a while, Tess lifted her head to look up into his eyes. 'And if I don't like it there?'

He was ready for that one. 'Then we stay here. I'll work in England. I'm never short of good offers over here,' he declared, without false modesty. 'There's enough that's interesting in this little country of yours— in the whole continent of Europe—to keep me busy till I'm an old, old man. In London, or anywhere in Britain. Wherever you want to be, Tess,' he said simply, 'that's the place I want to live.'

It was a sweeping statement; and she believed it. It seemed a solid proof of his love—almost the ultimate sacrifice for such a man. 'And if I do decide to sell up . . . come to New York with you,' she worked it out slowly, 'what would happen to Fritz?'

'He'd come with us, of course, anywhere we went. There are no quarantine laws in that direction—only coming back in. So you'd have to be very sure,' he warned. 'Bringing him back to England would be much more difficult. I'm sure you and Fritz would never put up with being apart for six months while he sweated it out in some kennels, where they won't spoil him in the manner to which he is accustomed. He'd pine away, and so would you.'

'You're jealous,' she accused. 'Jealous of a little cat!'

'Rubbish. I just know I can't have you without your mascot, that's all.' Josh kissed the tip of her nose. 'Will you do it, Tess? Come over and spend a real family Christmas with us? I can't wait for you to meet my parents—my sisters, and my nieces and nephews. You'll love them. And they'll love you,' he added firmly.

'How can you be so sure they'll love me?'

'They're bound to. *I* do.' He grinned wickedly. 'I just feel you'll like New Jersey, Tess. It's a very beautiful part of the States.'

Tess felt it too; but she wasn't ready to commit herself until she'd seen it. As for meeting the massed ranks of the Mayers and their in-laws, it sounded positively daunting! But she swallowed bravely. 'For you, Professor,' she said, 'I'll do it.'

'That's my girl!' He hugged her exuberantly. 'We'll have a great time—we always do.' Then he kissed her, deeply, lingeringly, until she clung to him, helpless as she always was when his mouth took possession of hers. 'And that,' he whispered, a little later,' is without benefit of mistletoe.' She had nothing to say in reply: actions spoke louder than words.

Quite a while later, Josh broke away as a thought occurred to him. 'What about Fritz?' he asked, his voice hoarse. 'Will he be okay by himself for a couple of weeks at Christmas?'

She warmed to him all over again for his genuine concern about her pet. 'He'll be fine. He loves Mrs Jacobs—she always looks after him when I go away. She's kinder to him than I am. She'll be heartbroken if I take him to America with me.'

'You could leave him with her?' Josh suggested.

'Not likely!' Realising he was teasing her, she subsided. 'I wouldn't leave Fritz, Josh. He's very special. He made a big difference to my life, all that time I was . . . alone. Just because I've got you now—and Danny— it doesn't mean I can forget what he's been to me over the years.'

'Quite right too. Shows commendable loyalty, Dr Hope. I applaud your sentiments.' He was deadly solemn. She tickled him under the ribs, but he refused to laugh. It wasn't fair: his self-control was impenetrable.

Danny opened one brown eye and regarded their antics with tolerant humour. He was getting used to this new angle on his father. He liked Tess a lot anyway—but if she was responsible for putting Josh into such a permanent good mood, she could stay around as long as she wanted, as far as he was concerned.

'Did you hear that, son?' Josh smiled across at him.

'What?' He smiled back, drowsy.

'Tess is going to live with us, very soon.'

'All the time?'

'All the time.'

'She won't go away, after . . . after she's been with us a while?'

'I won't ever go away, Danny,' Tess promised.

'Like—like having a mother?' he suggested tentatively.

'Exactly like that, Danny,' she confirmed.

'Then I'm glad.' He smiled; then his face fell. 'What about Fritz?'

'Fritz will live with us too,' said Josh. 'Wherever we live, he'll be there. The four of us will be there together. Okay?'

'Okay,' the little boy agreed, on a luxurious yawn. Then, one small hand resting on the cat's soft marmalade back, he fell asleep again.

Just what the woman on the go needs!

BOOKMATE

The perfect "mate" for all Harlequin paperbacks!

Holds paperbacks open for hands-free reading!

- TRAVELING
- VACATIONING
- AT WORK • IN BED
- COOKING • EATING
- STUDYING

Perfect size for all standard paperbacks, this wonderful invention makes reading a pure pleasure! Ingenious design holds paperback books OPEN and FLAT so even wind can't ruffle pages—leaves your hands free to do other things. Reinforced, wipe-clean vinyl-covered holder flexes to let you turn pages without undoing the strap...supports paperbacks so well, they have the strength of hardcovers!

Snaps closed for easy carrying.

Available now. Send your name, address, and zip or postal code, along with a check or money order for just $4.99 + .75¢ for postage & handling (for a total of $5.74) payable to Harlequin Reader Service to:

Harlequin Reader Service

In the U.S.A.
2504 West Southern Ave.
Tempe, AZ 85282

In Canada
P.O. Box 2800, Postal Station A
5170 Yonge Street,
Willowdale, Ont. M2N 5T5

MATE-1R

Share the joys and sorrows of real-life love with
Harlequin American Romance!™

GET THIS BOOK FREE as your introduction to Harlequin American Romance – an exciting series of romance novels written especially for the American woman of today.

Mail to:
Harlequin Reader Service

In the U.S.
2504 West Southern Ave.
Tempe, AZ 85282

In Canada
P.O. Box 2800, Postal Station A
5170 Yonge St., Willowdale, Ont. M2N 5T5

YES! I want to be one of the first to discover **Harlequin American Romance.** Send me FREE and without obligation *Twice in a Lifetime.* If you do not hear from me after I have examined my FREE book, please send me the 4 new **Harlequin American Romances** each month as soon as they come off the presses. I understand that I will be billed only $2.25 for each book (total $9.00). There are no shipping or handling charges. There is no minimum number of books that I have to purchase. In fact, I may cancel this arrangement at any time. *Twice in a Lifetime* is mine to keep as a FREE gift, even if I do not buy any additional books. 154-BPA-NAWD

Name _____ (please print)

Address _____ Apt. no. _____

City _____ State/Prov. _____ Zip/Postal Code _____

Signature (If under 18, parent or guardian must sign.)

This offer is limited to one order per household and not valid to current Harlequin American Romance subscribers. We reserve the right to exercise discretion in granting membership. If price changes are necessary, you will be notified.
Offer expires March 31, 1985

AMR-SUB-1